WISHES CAN COME TRUE

Meg Harper is shocked when the man she knows as Lucca Raffaele, who stood her up in Italy the previous summer, arrives to stay at her family home in Tennessee — this time calling himself her step-cousin, Jago Merryn ... Jago is there to acquire a local barbecue business, but discovering the woman who came close to winning his heart is only one of the surprises in store for him. Can they move past their mistrust and seize a second chance for their wishes to come true?

ANGELA BRITNELL

WISHES CAN COME TRUE

Complete and Unabridged

LINFORD
Leicester

First published in Great Britain in 2016

First Linford Edition
published 2017

A catalogue record for this book is available
from the British Library.

ISBN 978–1–4448–3470–3

Published by
F. A. Thorpe (Publishing)
Anstey, Leicestershire

Set by Words & Graphics Ltd.
Anstey, Leicestershire
Printed and bound in Great Britain by
T. J. International Ltd., Padstow, Cornwall

This book is printed on acid-free paper

1

Meg tiptoed into the kitchen and crept towards the back door.

'Make sure you're back for supper at six.' Her mother stopped in the middle of cooking pancakes. 'I want everyone here to meet your cousin.'

She could claim she had to work late. Or that poor Jago Merryn would be so jet-lagged he wouldn't appreciate a noisy welcome party. If she wanted to nitpick, she could call her mother out on declaring their guest to be a cousin. Strictly speaking, he was a step-cousin, because his mother only married into the family a couple of years ago. Her late grandfather Harper met his English bride while he was in the army and practising in Cornwall for the D-Day landings. After the war they'd settled there, and Jago's step-father Ernie was their youngest child.

But she said none of that. Betty Lou took her role as matriarch of the Harper family seriously, and was determined Jago would experience his fill of true southern hospitality when he flew into Nashville that afternoon.

'I'll be here,' Meg promised. 'But I'm afraid there won't be enough food for everyone to eat.' With a wry smile she glanced at the array of cooking spread out over the countertops. This was only her mother's effort, and the rest of the family would all turn up with their own contributions later. Aunt Sarah's potato salad, Uncle Joe's baked beans, and Cousin Martha's pecan pie — the list went on and on.

'Don't smart-talk me, young lady.'

'I wouldn't dare, Mother dear.' Meg popped a kiss on Betty Lou's cheek. 'Should I put on my best crinoline and sit on the porch when Daddy drives up with our visitor? I could whip up a few mint juleps if you like.'

'Get on with you.' Her mother smiled and shooed her away.

'I'll be on time. Promise.' Meg ran off before she could receive any more instructions and slammed the door behind her.

A big family get-together was the last thing she wanted to endure today. Hiding her work problems from the people who knew her well would be a challenge. Her only hope was that they'd be too busy fussing over their transatlantic relative to notice.

Don't be naive. The CIA could employ the Harper family as under-cover agents because they never missed anything that was going on around them.

Meg walked out to her car and mentally prepared herself for the day ahead.

★   ★   ★

Jago's short connecting flight from Charlotte seemed endless. When he wrapped up the job in Nashville, this was it for him — after a decade of travelling the world, the novelty had long since paled. His company acquisitions business was a huge success, and he was financially secure, but he'd paid a high price in his personal life and was ready to slow down.

As the plane started its descent, he took out the letter from Betty Lou Harper describing her husband who'd be meeting him. The Nashville airport was hardly Heathrow or Paris, but she was obviously afraid they'd miss each other.

He stowed everything back in his carry-on bag and raked his fingers through his hair, guessing it was a mess but unable to dredge up the energy to find a comb.

'Welcome to Nashville.' The loudspeaker greeting in the terminal by a big country music star left him in no doubt he'd arrived.

Jago spotted the burly, ruddy-faced man first and lifted his hand to wave. Grayson Harper was well into his sixties and had worked outdoors all his life, judging by his walnut skin and the creases fanning out across his face.

'Hello, sir.'

'Call me Gray. Everyone does.' He checked out Jago's paltry amount of luggage. 'Travelling light?' He chuckled. 'Meg would need that bag for her shoes.'

'Meg?'

'My daughter. Got a couple of boys too.'

'Quite a family. I haven't been around much since my mother and Ernie married, so I'm not up to speed on all of you.'

'They're good kids.' The man beamed. 'They'll be around for supper later.'

Jago plastered on a smile.

'I told Betty Lou you'd be tired, but she cracked the whip, and no one disobeys her if they're smart.'

Jago heard the warning in the friendly words and dutifully expressed his pleasure at the idea of meeting the whole Harper family in one fell swoop.

'Come on, let's get out of this mess.' Gray glanced at his watch. 'We should avoid the worst of rush hour.'

'How far is it to your house?'

'About forty minutes.'

'Let's do it.' Jago picked up his duffel bag and backpack. He followed Gray out of the small terminal building and a welcome blast of hot air hit his face. When he left Cornwall, it'd been cool and rainy despite the fact it was June and supposed to be summer. He'd inherited a lot of his Italian father's Mediterranean characteristics and always felt more alive in warm climates.

'I'm not gonna be offended if you fall asleep on the way. You'll need all your strength when the women start yacking at you.' Gray chuckled. He opened the door of an ancient pick-up truck. Jago guessed the paint had been red at one time, but most of the colour visible now was pure rust.

'Good plan.' He hopped in and shifted the passenger seat back to accommodate his long legs. Jago could sleep anywhere and at any time. He'd honed the skill years ago and it'd proved invaluable. Often he'd been underestimated by business contacts after a long journey when they'd expected him to be sluggish and jet-lagged, only to be proved woefully wrong. The Harper family weren't a billion-dollar takeover bid, but it wouldn't do any harm to have his brain turned on when he met them.

A deep voice penetrated Jago's brain and he stirred. 'We're here. This road leads up to Red Roof Farm.' Gray laughed. 'Not an imaginative man, my great-grandfather.'

Jago woke up enough to look out of the window. 'He was practical.' The outbuildings on either side of the one-land gravel road all had the required red roofs and the well-maintained white fences around the property, and the lush, pristine land-scape gave it a completely different feel to the wild beauty of Cornwall. The first flash of interest stirred in him and Jago smiled. Every time he arrived in a new place he felt a keenness to experience another culture. Even on short trips, he made time to get away from the luxury hotels and stuffy offices.

'It's a neat place.'

'Yeah, it sure is.' Gray's pride in his land was obvious. 'Here's the house.'

They parked and Jago ran his gaze over the sprawling building. He'd expected the classic white-painted wood exterior, red roof, and wrap-around porch complete with rocking chairs, but not the hundreds of people swarming all over the place. *Don't exaggerate.* At a quick count he guessed at least fifty people were there to meet him.

'Looks like the gang's all here,' Gray observed. 'You ready?'

'Lead me to the slaughter.' Jago cracked a smile and threw open the truck door.

A tall brunette stepped off of the

porch, and he automatically checked out her long jeans-clad legs and tempting curves. As his gaze reached her face, Jago's stomach dropped and he considered turning around and getting right back in the truck. But something propelled him forward, and he caught a brief flash of anger in the woman's wide gray eyes before the shutters came down.

'Welcome to Red Roof Farm, Mr. Merryn.' Her emphasis on his name made Jago wince, and for once in his life he was lost for words.

2

You can do this, Meg told herself as she went through the motions of greeting their English guest. A myriad of questions raced through her head, mostly along the lines of why the man standing in front of her was calling himself Jago Merryn, and whether he needed to look as appealing as she remembered. Today's dark jeans and casual blue-and-white checked shirt were very different from the designer suit she'd last seen him wearing, but everything else was the same — from the black wavy hair curling over his collar, to his smooth tanned skin and deep-set dark eyes.

'Come on in and meet everyone.' Meg didn't shake his hand or give him the traditional southern hug.

'Meg, love, what are you thinking?' Her mother jumped in and pulled Jago into a tight hug before letting go. 'Come and see your room. You've got thirty minutes to freshen up, and by then the guys will have the burgers ready.'

Despite everything, Meg smiled at her mother's mixture of warmth and military precision. Betty Lou was the reason the Harper household ran as smoothly as a well-greased wheel.

'Thank you, Mrs. Harper. You're very kind to have me to stay.'

'Call me Betty Lou. You're family.' She shepherded him up the steps. 'Meg, take Jago with you and show him where everything is. I need to get back in the kitchen before your Aunt Sarah ruins my coleslaw. She'll try to sneak in that darned red cabbage your daddy hates.'

Meg knew better than to argue. 'I'd be happy to.' She aimed a fake smile at Jago. 'Follow me.'

She explained the history of the house as they walked through to the annex at the back. The first building on

Red Roof land had been a wood cabin erected by her great-great grandfather in the 1860s, and after that came this house. Meg didn't give Jago any chance to ask questions, personal or otherwise. They reached his rooms and stopped outside the door.

'My mother redid this part last year, so you should be comfortable.'

'Meghan, I — '

She cut off his attempt to speak: 'Please don't say any more.' A flash of heat raced up his neck. 'I'll show you where everything is, and then I need to get back to help out.'

He nodded and remained silent while she gave him the rundown on the vagaries of the shower and showed him the large bedroom and living room he had for his own use.

'That door opens onto the backyard, and you'll find a table and a couple of chairs out there. Our Wi-Fi is fairly reliable, and the cell phone reception isn't bad.' She managed another smile. 'I'll see you back out on the porch when you're ready to face the mob.'

Meg swiftly walked away, but he spoke her name again as she reached the door. His warm gaze rested on her and unwelcome memories flooded back, making her throat tighten. 'I understand this isn't the right time, but I intend to explain . . . things to you.'

'Don't bother. It doesn't matter now,' she insisted, and walked out.

Jago made no attempt to stop her. Of all the women he'd expected to see today, Meghan Simpson hadn't made the list. He'd known she came from somewhere near Nashville, but had no reason to connect her with the Harper family.

He unzipped his duffel bag and unpacked before stripping off and turning the shower on full blast. Plainly Meghan wouldn't talk to him any more than she could help, but he might be able to use his well-honed people skills to find out her story from the rest of the family.

Five minutes later he stretched out

on the bed and told himself to take a ten-minute nap. It was one of his quirkier talents and even worked over a change in time zones. Jago listened to the ceiling fan and took several long, slow breaths.

The sound of children playing outside his window penetrated his consciousness and he opened one eye to check the clock. Nine minutes and fifty-five seconds. Not bad. He got up and tugged on a pair of black shorts and a T-shirt bearing the Cornish flag. Putting on a pair of flip-flops, he ran his fingers through his hair to settle down the waves. Then he hitched a pair of sunglasses on the neck of his shirt and slipped his phone in his pocket before opening the door.

'Are you the English guy?' A freckle-faced little boy gave Jago a hard stare. 'Say something.'

'Why?'

'Gran-gran told us you talk funny.'

Jago was sure Betty Lou hadn't expected that gem to be repeated.

'Sounds to me as though you're the one who talks funny.'

The boy realised he was being teased and grinned, exposing the gap where his new front teeth would be. 'You wanna go eat?'

'I certainly do. I'm starving. Is there anything good?'

'Tons.' The boy frowned. 'But they won't let us eat until you come. Hurry up.' He tugged on Jago's hand.

'Do you have a name?' he asked as they walked through the house.

'Of course I do.' The scornful reply implied the boy couldn't believe anyone was that stupid. 'It's Cody Ford Harper. My daddy is Cooper Edison Harper and my mommy is Beth Anne Richardson Harper. My grandfather — '

'Good to meet you, Cody.' The kid would recite the whole genealogy of the Harper family if he wasn't careful. 'Lead me to the hamburgers.'

'Sure thing.' Cody beamed and let go of his hand to race ahead. He opened the screen door onto the porch and yelled: 'I found him.'

Jago stepped out onto the wooden deck and spotted Meghan bending over an ice cooler. She straightened up, and two circles of bright red heat coloured her cheeks.

Betty Lou appeared by his side. 'Come with me; you must be starving. You'll eat first and then meet everyone. Say grace, Gray,' she shouted over to her husband, who was busy flipping burgers on an oversized grill; and he did as he was told, racing through a quick prayer. 'Y'all hang on while I get this boy fed,' Betty Lou told the rest of the family, and Jago didn't argue as she pulled him along in her wake. Down on the lawn in front of the house, two long tables were set up in the shade of a massive oak tree.

Jago struggled to take in everything Betty Lou told him about who made which dish, but gave up. He'd better try everything, he decided, because he didn't want to hurt anyone's feelings.

'Load up your plate and sit with me on the porch; I'm taking first chance to talk to you,' Betty Lou said firmly. 'Gray, get those burgers over here now.'

'Yes, ma'am.'

Jago suppressed a smile at Gray's brisk response, and in a matter of seconds the older man ran over with a platter of sizzling hamburgers.

Soon Jago was ensconced in one of the rocking chairs with Betty Lou next to him. 'Beer, water or soda?' she asked.

'I'd better stick with water tonight or I'll be fast asleep before I can manage to eat all this good food.'

Betty Lou nodded her approval. 'Meg, bring us two bottles of water.'

Meg's shoulders stiffened, but she smiled and returned to the ice cooler. 'There you are.' She handed them over and quickly left them alone.

'Dig in, and then tell me all about yourself and catch me up with the family news,' Betty Lou ordered.

He should have stayed at a hotel in Nashville as he'd originally planned,

Jago thought. Now he'd have to watch what he was saying to protect Meg from her mother's inquisitive nature. He opened his water and took a long, deep drink before picking up his loaded plate. It was time to get creative.

3

Meg skirted around the side of the house to avoid her Aunt Sarah, who'd been trying to pigeonhole her all the afternoon.

Her father appeared, brandishing a plate of food and holding out a can of soda. 'Hiding from the family inquisition? Here, I thought you could do with this.'

'Thanks.' Meg took the offerings from him and pulled out one of the patio chairs to sit down. 'You going to snatch a few minutes' peace too?'

'Better not or your mama will be after my tail,' he joked.

A shard of unadulterated envy shot through her. She didn't want to care about approaching thirty without any prospect of finding the sort of love her parents shared, but some days it was hard not to wonder.

'Is everything all right at work?'

'Fine. Busy, but I like that.' Meg's strident assurance sounded harsh to her own ears, and her father's shrewd stare told her he wasn't fooled. If he knew that the money she'd invested in a local barbeque sauce company was at risk, he'd offer to help out, but she'd taken the chance in the first place and must get through it on her own.

'You know you can always come to me, don't you?'

'Of course, Daddy.' Meg blinked back tears.

'Come back when you're ready. Your mama is starting to wonder where you are, and the kids want you to play some games with them.'

Normally she loved hanging out with the little ones, but wasn't sure she could face it today. Her father began to walk away but stopped and glanced back over his shoulder.

'Jago strikes me as a good man, and the women are lapping him up out there. You'd think he was the Duke of

Whatever-it-is on that dumb show your mom watches.'

'He's hardly *Downton Abbey* material, but seems pleasant enough.' She hoped her comment struck the right balance between friendly and interested. Meg didn't intend to be either of those things with Jago Merryn, or whatever he was calling himself today, but her father didn't need to know that.

Meg was left alone with her thoughts.

⋆ ⋆ ⋆

Jago tried to fix everyone's names and their places in the family tree in his brain.

'This is my sister Sarah,' Betty Lou explained. 'She'll talk your ear off.' His hostess brushed off the other woman's attempt to protest and rushed away to separate two of the youngest Harpers, who were fighting.

'Sit down, boy, and let me look at you.' Sarah pointed a spindly finger at him. 'You're a good-looking fellow.

21

They say you're not married. Why not?'

'I could ask you the same, but I'm far too well-mannered. Let's just say I'm choosy too.'

Her stony glare dissipated and she broke into a loud cackling laugh. 'You'd do well for our Meg,' she pronounced.

'Meg? Trying to marry her off, are you?'

'The girl's not getting any younger.'

Jago thanked his lucky stars that his own family mostly stayed out of his personal life. Apart from his mother's occasional comment about wanting grandchildren before she was too old to play with them, Jago went his own way.

'She's been good friends with the Docherty boy for years, and he'd marry her in a heartbeat, but they wouldn't suit. She'd trample all over him.' Sarah scoffed.

'Does Meg work in Nashville?'

'She does public relations for a local company.'

So Ms. Meghan Harper wasn't the artisan leather designer she'd claimed to be in Florence. He wasn't the only one who'd skirted around the truth. 'I'm sure she's doing well,' he ventured.

'She's back living here though, isn't she?'

'Maybe she enjoys being around her family.' Jago couldn't think of anything worse himself, but everyone was different.

'Don't talk nonsense, young man. Even I got out from under my parents' feet as soon as I could, wedding ring or no wedding ring. Do you live with yours?'

'No.'

'Didn't think so.'

It was time to change the subject. 'I loved your potato salad. Will you give me the recipe?'

'No, I won't. The family has tried to pry it out of me for years. And don't try fluttering those long lashes because I'm too old to fall for that trick. Better men than you have tried and failed.'

They probably gave up to keep their masculinity intact.

'Leave me alone now to take a nap in peace.'

Jago prised himself out of the small wicker chair. 'It's been a pleasure to meet you.'

'Did you find out what you wanted?'

'I certainly did, and thank you very much.'

Sarah's eyes gleamed. 'As I said before, you'd do well for our Meg. But if you hurt her you'll have us to deal with.' She waved her hand over the assembled family.

Jago didn't make any comment and hurried to leave before she could start on him again. His childhood had taught him the danger of caring too much, and one date in Florence had showed him that Meg could be a danger to his heart. He wandered along the porch and decided against joining in with the games going on in the field next to the house. He had work to do before he turned up at Mama Belle's Barbecue Sauce Company tomorrow morning and needed to get a good night's sleep.

He spotted Meg and watched her for a few moments. She ran after little Cody and swung him up in her arms, laughing and tickling him until he pleaded for mercy. A shaft of remembrance tunnelled through Jago of walking hand in hand with her along the banks of the Arno River. He'd kissed her on the doorstep of her hotel, one lingering sweet kiss, and had wanted so much more. Instead he'd deliberately chosen to let her go.

Jago decided to find Betty Lou and plead tiredness to escape to his cool, quiet rooms. The sooner he got on a plane back to London, the better it would be for him and Meg both.

4

Meg crept downstairs and hoped her nemesis wasn't an early riser. She was happy to skip breakfast, but needed her coffee before she could face the drive to work.

'Oh, you're up already,' she said, her heart sinking as she entered the kitchen.

Typical, Jago thought as he leaned against the kitchen counter brandishing a mug in one hand and a toasted bagel in the other. He glanced down over himself and back up to her, his warm brown eyes dancing with amusement. 'I'd have to say I am.'

His casual look of yesterday was gone, replaced with an immaculate dark suit, crisp white shirt, silk tie, and polished shoes. Along with a perfect clean shave and his hair slicked close to his head and gleaming under the fluorescent lights,

Jago looked the part — at least whatever part he was playing now.

'Where are you working in Nashville, anyway?' Meg asked him. 'Your step-father was vague when he called to say you were coming.'

'He was vague because I didn't tell him.' He picked a stray thread off his suit jacket. 'The people I do business with don't appreciate publicity until the deal is wrapped up.'

'What on earth do you do? I'm taking a wild guess it's not math teaching.'

A touch of heat coloured his cheeks but his gaze remained steady. 'No. And a little birdie told me yesterday that you're not a handbag designer either, so we're equal in the untruthfulness stakes.'

She'd almost forgotten the job she'd plucked out of the air when they met.

'My business deals in company acquisitions,' he explained.

'So you buy up failing businesses cheap, sell them on and make a fortune?'

By the way his eyes darkened, Jago

didn't care for her sharp summary of his work. Meg became aware of two things. Firstly, she'd been inexcusably rude to a guest — something her mother would never forgive. Secondly, and far worse, her short dressing gown revealed far too much of her legs, and the quirk of amusement pulling at the corners of his mouth told her Jago had noticed.

'I'd better get ready for work,' she muttered.

'Unless it's a very casual Monday, I'd reluctantly have to agree.'

She ignored his flirtatious banter and grabbed a mug from the table before filling it up from the coffee pot. Meg heard a car horn outside and Jago straightened up, his smile fading.

'That'll be my limo. I'll be off. You can enjoy your breakfast in peace.' He headed for the door. 'I'll see you tonight. I'd better go and see if I can save another business from bankruptcy.' He strode off, and an intoxicating mix of soap and expensive cologne lingered in the air. Lucca Raffaele smelled exactly as Meg remembered.

★ ★ ★

Jago leaned back in the plush leather seat and closed his eyes, but Meg filled his brain and wouldn't leave him alone. The real problem wasn't the physical pull between them, but the way she sparked off of him, exactly as he remembered. At thirty-five, he hadn't met another woman to compare with Meghan Simpson — or Harper, as she really was. He'd been enjoying some down time in Florence after finalising another successful deal, and Meg had literally flung herself at his feet. She'd tripped on the uneven pavement while trying to rescue her handbag from one of the notorious moped thieves. After making sure she was okay, he'd taken off running and yanked the teenager off his bike when he slowed down for a traffic jam. Meghan had called Jago her hero, and he hadn't been able to refuse her offer of taking him out to dinner as a gesture of thanks.

Why he'd said he was a math teacher, Jago couldn't imagine, but it'd been the first thing that came to mind when she asked what he did for a living. Women were often only interested in his money, and it made him cautious. Anyway, what was the point of telling her the truth? She wouldn't care to hear why he'd stood her up the second night. Why should she?

'Nearly there, sir. Traffic's not bad this morning,' Ron, the chauffeur, said, and Jago managed a polite response. He needed to focus on today's main task and put the rest to one side.

'Good. I'll be here all day, Ron. Is it all right if I call you half an hour before I want to leave?'

'Yes, sir. I'll be here.' He eased the car to a stop.

'Thanks.' Jago got out and stood still for a moment to run his eye over the building's neo-classical facade. He'd guess it had been built in the 1950s, and from what he'd read, most of the company's business practices dated back to then as well. The barbecue sauce company that'd once been a leader in the southeast was struggling.

He made his way up the steps and took note of the dull brasswork around the door and faded black paint. Small points, but an indication of slipping standards. Jago pressed the bell and heard footsteps on the other side of the door before it opened.

'Mr Merryn?'

Jago couldn't blame the short red-faced man for looking wary. 'Pleased to meet you, Mr — '

'Clayborne Williams. Senior partner. My late father-in-law, Bucky Owen, started the company.' He ushered Jago inside. 'Everyone's in the boardroom upstairs to meet you — the plant manager and one of the more junior managers who's on her way are the only people who don't know the reason for your visit. I figured I'd let you do the explaining.' Clayborne glanced over

Jago's shoulder. 'We expected you to bring people with you.'

Jago's legal and financial officers had already done their work, and he preferred to fly solo for the final negotiations. 'No, it's just me.' Jago wanted to get on with this. 'Shall we start?'

They made their way up a long winding staircase, and although he was impressed by the elegant building, Jago didn't see why a barbecue sauce company needed a historic downtown building for its headquarters. This edifice should fetch a decent amount of money to offset the huge debts, and he'd put it on the market as soon as the ink was dry on their agreement.

'Here we all are.' Williams opened back a pair of ornate carved wood doors, and the group of gray-suited men stared openly at them. Williams introduced the senior partners and the plant manager before making his way down to a tall, lanky man about Jago's age. 'This is Elliott Docherty, our junior partner. He's a grandson of John Bell

32

Porter, one of our founders.'

Jago shook the man's hand on automatic pilot while his mind raced over Aunt Sarah's story about Meg's longtime best friend. This was bad luck. 'Could you take me out to your factory later?'

'He'd be delighted. Wouldn't you, Elliott?' Mr. Williams jumped in.

'Of course.' Elliott's charming smile was at odds with his clenched jaw and taut posture.

'I'd like us all to meet back here first thing tomorrow ready to start serious negotiations,' Jago said.

'You won't need any longer to size things up?' Williams asked.

'That shouldn't be necessary. I don't intend to drag things out.'

'I'm sorry I'm late. Traffic was a nightmare.' Meg breezed into the room, and her brief horror as she registered Jago's presence was quickly replaced by a cool smile.

Jago stood frozen to the spot, completely struck dumb.

5

'Miss Harper, this is Mr. Jago Merryn from London. He's come to discuss a possible takeover and acquisition of the company.'

Meg plastered her hands to her sides and managed a grim smile. 'Am I the only one who didn't know about this?'

'The decision was made to wait and inform all non-voting board members today,' Williams explained.

'I put my life savings into this business. Doesn't that count for anything?' Meg fixed her glare on Elliott. When the business was struggling he'd turned to her for assistance, pleading with her to help them get back on track. She'd been tired of working in a large public relations company in Knoxville and seized the opportunity to return to Nashville. She'd spent the last year metaphorically banging her head against a brick wall while the senior partners refused to make any changes.

'I'm sorry, Meg. I wanted to warn you, but . . . ' Elliot's voice trailed away.

You didn't have the courage, she thought angrily.

'Miss Harper . . . ' Jago cleared his throat. 'There will be compensation packages for all board members and employees. Remember we don't have an agreement yet. This could all fall through.'

Meg was determined not to roll over and play dead until there was no choice.

'We're meeting again tomorrow after I've visited the factory with Mr. Docherty.'

The thought of losing everything and going back to square one again overwhelmed her. 'I'll be in my office.' Forcing herself to walk instead of run, she made her escape.

★ ★ ★

Somehow she got through the day without seeing Jago again. She'd go home, snatch a quick bite to eat, and hole up in her bedroom to work on a Christmas present for her mother. Betty Lou always complained she couldn't find anything in her voluminous totebags, and Meg had an idea for one with fun labels and a multitude of brightly coloured pockets. She might not do leatherwork, but did enjoy sewing and made a lot of her own clothes. If they were racking up scores, she was pretty sure Jago's lie about being a math teacher ranked higher on the dishonesty scale.

Half an hour later she arrived at Red Roof Farm and discovered a brief note from her mother to say they were out visiting friends. Meg changed out of her business suit into an ankle-length summer dress she'd made from white voile material splashed with huge scarlet poppies, a bargain in an end-of-season sale. She added a pair of red flip-flops and made her way back down to the kitchen.

Cooking wasn't her favourite pastime, but her mother kept a well-stocked fridge

— one of the few benefits of living at home. Meg found some cold chicken and the remains of a couple of salads from yesterday's party and dished herself up a generous plate of food. Along with a large glass of sweet tea, she was all set.

Out on the patio, the sun had started to go down, and a welcome breeze cooled her skin. Meg bit into a chicken leg and didn't stop until she'd eaten every scrap.

Jago suddenly appeared in front of her. 'Don't they feed you at work?'

'Oddly enough, I didn't have much of an appetite at lunchtime.'

An angry red flush crept up his neck. 'I'm sorry.'

'Yeah, I'm sure you are.'

'That's a pretty dress.'

'Thank you.' Meg struggled to be polite. 'How was the rest of your day?'

'I'm happy to chat, but do you mind if I change out of all this first?' He gestured at his suit. 'Then I'll come back to join you.'

'Feel free. There's plenty of food in the fridge. Help yourself.' Betty Lou would be a good hostess and offer to get him something to eat, but Meg didn't move an inch. Why should she?

Jago couldn't help feeling sorry for her. If he'd known a member of the Harper family was involved with his deal, he wouldn't have chosen to stay here and might have given the whole acquisition a wide berth. *What you really mean is you wouldn't have touched anything connected to the captivating Meg in a month of Sundays.*

He retreated to his rooms and ditched his hated suit. When he quit being the public face of JLM Industries, he swore to himself he'd never wear another suit and tie to work again. After a cool shower, he put on his favourite crumpled linen shorts and Rolling Stones T-shirt. Black flip-flops. Sunglasses. Hair shaken out of its neat daytime style, and a splash of cologne. All armour to face Meg again.

The pork barbecue sandwich he'd had at lunchtime was only a distant memory, so he headed straight for the kitchen, where he loaded up his plate with leftovers and found a knife and fork before grabbing a beer from the fridge. He popped the top open and took a long, deep swallow.

Meg appeared in the doorway. 'I came on a cookie search and . . . '

'And?'

'I felt guilty about leaving you to find your own dinner, and in my head I heard my mother telling me off.'

'She's quite a woman.'

'My dad calls her a force of nature.'

Jago nodded. 'Smart man.' He lifted up his plate. 'As you can see, I'm not helpless, and am very good at sniffing out food.'

Meg opened a plastic box on the counter and held it out to him. 'Help yourself. They're homemade, but not by me, so you're safe.'

'Cooking isn't your thing?'

'Nope. Only when I'm forced to. It's

one benefit to living at home.'

Jago chuckled. 'It wouldn't be if we were talking about my mother.'

'She's not a gourmet cook?'

'Nobody with an ounce of sense puts her name and the word 'cook' in the same sentence.'

Meg scoffed. 'I bet you're exaggerating.'

He launched into the story of his mother's ban from bringing anything homemade to the church bake sale again after someone broke a tooth on one of her flapjacks. 'She misread the recipe and cooked it for three hours instead of thirty minutes.'

A wide smile lit up Meg's face. 'At least I haven't caused bodily harm yet with my cooking.'

Jago added a couple of cookies to his plate. 'That should keep body and soul together for a few hours.'

'I wouldn't want you to fade away.'

Wouldn't you? He held her gaze, and for a few seconds the connection they'd made in Italy flooded back and grabbed him by the throat. 'It would make things easier, wouldn't it?' he murmured.

'Come on.' She jerked away, breaking the moment.

Just as well, he thought.

They settled on the patio and didn't say much for a while as they concentrated on eating.

'Would you care for another beer?'

'No, thanks,' Jago said with a grin. 'That's not the truth — I'd love one, but I've got work to do and don't need my brain to be fuzzy.'

'Oh, yes, work. Need to be sharp for that, don't we?'

'You didn't mention where you worked.' He tried not to sound resentful. 'I know I've not been honest either, but I did explain the reason behind that.'

Meg shrugged. 'Don't worry. We don't do honesty. Do we?'

There was nothing he could easily say to her question.

'I'll be a well-brought-up southern

lady and change the subject. We'll go back to talking about beer and your self-restraint. I admire your discipline.'

'It's got me where I am today.'

'Which is?'

'Financially secure and at the point where I can draw back. This is hopefully the last deal I'll oversee personally. I've been on the road one way and another for the last thirteen years. I'm more than ready for a break.'

'Do you have somewhere to go home to?'

Jago took a large bite of his cookie.

'Sorry. I didn't mean to be too personal.' She touched his hand.

'Meg, dear, where are you?' her mother's shrill voice rang out, and Jago instinctively jerked away.

6

'There you both are. I was just going on a search for this boy. Did you find something to eat? I figured you'd work something out,' Betty Lou rattled on, and Meg didn't dare to look at Jago.

'We're doing fine, thank you,' he said. 'Meg's been taking good care of me.'

Her mother beamed. 'I'm goin' to put the coffee on and then we'll come join you. The Tylers only served fruit for dessert, and you know your daddy won't last the evening if he doesn't get his sugar fix. He's washing his hands and he'll be out in a minute.'

As soon as Betty Lou disappeared, Meg sneaked a quick look at Jago.

'Don't worry about me. I'll survive.' He gave her arm a gentle prod. 'I'm tough.'

Something tells me you've had to be. All she knew was that a couple of years

43

ago Uncle Ernie suddenly up and got himself married despite everyone's assumption that he was a confirmed bachelor. His new wife, Cecily, was a divorcée with one grown-up son, but the family knew nothing else about her.

'I honestly need to do some work.' Jago pushed the chair back and stood up. 'Will you make my excuses to your parents?'

'Of course. I'll see you tomorrow.'

'Not if I see you first.' The laughter in his voice didn't reach his eyes, but she played along and smiled back. Something about Jago got to her, and it wasn't simply his good looks. It'd been the same way in Florence when he became her knight in shining armour. She'd offered to take him out for dinner as a reward, and his rich brown eyes had darkened to an intense shade of black.

'Perfect. Dinner tonight. And a kiss,' he'd whispered against her cheek.

He'd taken hold of her hand to walk her safely back to her hotel. Later they'd spent a magical evening together that had ended in an incredible kiss outside her hotel. She'd been committed to going sightseeing the next day with her friends, but Jago promised to pick her up in the evening for another date. But he hadn't turned up, and sent no explanation. Until yesterday, Meg wondered if she'd imagined him — but Jago, or Lucca as she still thought of him, was only too real.

And back to stir you up all over again. If she valued her heart, she dare not let him.

★ ★ ★

Jago exhaled a sigh of relief. Thank goodness the Hardings had returned and saved him from making a fool of himself. Meg had touched his heart in Italy and threatened to do the same now. The sooner he got his work done and left, the better it would be for them both. But his success could ruin her financially, or at the very least cost Meg her job.

Elliott had told him that afternoon that he and a couple of the younger partners were trying to raise enough money to counter Jago's bid. The man had revealed a different side when they'd toured the small rundown factory, and spoken almost poetically about the sauce his grandfather invented. At one point there had been several factories spread throughout the south, but as business diminished they'd gradually closed until the Nashville factory was the only one remaining. The company still owned the other buildings and land, which was what made them an attractive proposition to Jago.

He stretched out on the bed with his laptop and started to work, but several taps on the door stirred him from his calculations.

'Gray. Is something up?'

Meg's father gave him a sheepish smile. 'Only my stubborn wife. Meg told us you had work to do, but Betty

Lou refuses to believe her.' He tossed up his hands in the air. 'She insists we'd be failing in our family duty if we didn't feed you dessert.'

Jago laughed. 'Don't fret. I'll come and join you for a while, but I really do have work to finish up later.'

'Women. Can't live with 'em and can't live without 'em.'

Jago wasn't touching that minefield.

'They've got coffee made, and Betty Lou dug up a cake from somewhere too, because she thinks cookies aren't much to offer you.'

'Neither of you saw how much I already ate,' Jago teased. 'I'll have to go for a run in the morning as a preventative measure.'

When they stepped out onto the patio, he noticed Meg's colour rise, but she didn't look directly at him.

'Sit by me.' Betty Lou patted the chair next to her. 'I want to hear what you've been up to today.'

'Mom,' Meg pleaded, 'remember what I said. He can't talk about the work he's doing.'

Jago guessed her family didn't know about the problems at Mama Belle's, and he didn't intend to spill her secret. They'd find out soon enough.

'Nonsense. We're family. We aren't going to blab.'

'Betty Lou.' The serious edge to Gray's voice surprised Jago. She instantly fell quiet. Gray might not say a lot, but when he did his wife listened.

'I'm enjoying what I've seen of Nashville so far,' Jago said, trying to distract his hostess. 'Have you always lived in this part of Tennessee?' The question set her off, and Jago sipped his coffee while listening to a long story about the generations of Harpers and Simpsons who'd settled the area back in the early 1800s.

'There aren't many of what I call 'old Franklin' people who aren't related to us somewhere along the line. I can usually find a connection, and if someone is kinfolk they're usually decent.' Betty Lou nodded sagely. 'What about your people, Jago? Tell me about them.'

'My father was born in Sicily and came to work in Cornwall at one of the tourist hotels. He met my mother and they married and settled there. They had me fairly quickly, but things didn't work out between them.' That was a massive understatement, but the most he intended to say. The bitter arguments and multiple times his father had left home and threatened not to come back were etched deeply in his mind. The year Jago turned sixteen, his father had left for good, and his parents quietly divorced.

'That was hard on you,' Betty Lou murmured. 'I can't imagine what it's like not to have that bedrock of a family to support you.'

'My mother has always been there for me.' As a teenager he'd resented her for not standing up to his father more, but with the benefit of age he understood that apart from panda bears, zebras and newspapers, most things weren't black and white.

'After the divorce my mother reverted to her maiden name of Merryn, and I started to use it too. I was surprised when she remarried, but Ernie's a decent man.'

'He sure is. Ernie came over here for our wedding back in the dark ages,' Betty Lou recalled with a smile. 'My sister had her eye on him then, but her outspokenness scared the poor man off. Your mother must be a special lady, because I never thought he'd willingly go down the aisle.'

'You'd like her. She's very different from Ernie. She talks everyone's ear off, and I don't think she's ever met a stranger. Ernie adores her.'

'I hope we get to meet her one day.' Betty Lou's smile brightened. 'If you don't have any plans for the weekend, Meg could show you around the local area. You won't be leaving before then, will you?'

'I shouldn't think so.'

'That's settled, then.'

Gray caught his eye and Jago struggled to suppress a laugh. The man had been right — his wife truly was an unstoppable force.

'If Meg doesn't have anything else on her agenda, I'd be delighted.' He caught Meg's eye.

'I'll see how things are by Friday, okay?'

'Fair enough.' Jago stood up. 'I'd prefer to stay here talking, but I have things to get ready for the morning.' He gave an apologetic smile. 'This time you really *will* have to excuse me.'

Betty Lou opened her mouth, but Gray shook his head and she subsided back into the chair.

'I'm going as well.' Meg jumped up and headed for the door.

Jago ran ahead and opened it for her. 'Thanks.'

'What for?'

'Not bursting your mother's bubble. Don't worry — I won't hold you to being my tour guide.'

Meg's enigmatic gray eyes took on a sparkling silvery hue. 'I might not mind. I'll see.' With that, she walked away and left him with his mouth gaping open.

7

Today Meg had made sure to get up early and escape from the house before she bumped into Jago. What had possessed her to say such a thing to him last night? At work she closed her office door and did a couple of hours of solid work. She put together several press releases and an idea for a television commercial, all the while wondering why she was wasting her time. When Elliott talked her into joining him at Mama Belle's, he'd convinced her the company could be a gold mine with a change of direction. She'd seen herself as crucial in the modernisation until she realised the older directors weren't interested in doing anything to upset the status quo.

Meg glanced up at the clock and realised it was nearly noon. The summer heat didn't bother her, so she'd change her shoes and take a walk along the river. She hadn't taken the time to pack a lunch that morning, but there would be plenty of food vendors around, and for once she'd indulge.

After a brisk half-mile or so, she reached Riverfront Park, and the tempting aromas from a hot-dog cart broke her resolve to choose something healthy. With her chilli dog and an ice-cold bottle of water, she settled down on the grass and watched the people around her. A mixture of tourists and office workers were making the most of the day's lower humidity and slight breeze off the river.

'I should've known you'd be in your favourite spot.' The sound of Elliott's good-humoured voice made Meg turn around.

'Have you escaped the grindstone too?'

'Yeah, you could say that. But we might not have a grindstone to escape from soon, which makes things worse.'

Elliott dropped down to sit beside her. His usually sunny smile was absent, and deep worry lines creased his forehead. 'Merryn seemed decent enough when I showed him around the factory, but the man's an iceberg over the negotiations. He's not shifting an inch.' Elliott shook his head. 'I'm sorry I dragged you into all this. I honestly thought it'd be a great move for you and help out the business.'

Meg squeezed his hand. 'It's not your fault.' She couldn't be cross with him because they'd been friends far too long. For a second she considered mentioning her family connection with the Merryn family but held back. Elliott might misinterpret her relationship with Jago, and they didn't need that complication on top of everything else. 'I've been working on some ideas, but I'm not sure the others will want to listen.'

'I'm not either. I think the older guys see this as a chance to retire with a tidy pot of money. They'll do all right out of it but we won't, plus our jobs will disappear. I feel I'm letting my grandfather down.'

'You're doing everything you can.' She didn't know how to encourage him without lying about their prospects of saving the company.

'Maybe.' Elliott's blue eyes pierced through her. 'If you can come up with a bright idea to see off Mr. Merryn and his money, plus save the business, I'll be eternally grateful.'

'I'll give it my best shot.'

His warm gaze rested on her. 'I know. You give a hundred percent to everything you do. It's one of the many things I've always admired about you.' He ruffled her hair. 'I've got to get back.' He stood up. 'Let me know if you have any brainwaves.'

'I will.' Meg swallowed hard. 'We'll get together soon.' He nodded and walked away, leaving her deep in thought.

★ ★ ★

Jago clenched his hands. It'd tested his self-control to stand in the shadow of a large tree and watch Elliott and Meg together. Earlier at the office Elliott had mentioned the riverfront, and when they had a break from negotiations Jago turned down everyone's offers of lunch to escape for a much-needed walk. Maybe her Aunt Sarah was wrong and Meg *did* return Elliott's admiration.

You don't do commitment. Remember? It shouldn't matter to you how she feels.

He started to walk back along the path before Meg could spot him, but a nagging headache pulled at his temples. Jago wished he could go back to Red Roof Farm and lie down. The idea of another afternoon spent trying to convince Clayborne Williams and the rest of the group that he wasn't out to fleece them held no appeal.

Before he could change his mind, Jago phoned Ron and asked him to pick him up near the Ghost Ballet sculpture in about twenty minutes. He'd read it was officially called the 'Ghost Ballet for the East Bank Machineworks' to reflect the city's industrial past, but the locals commonly referred to it as the big red roller coaster. The sculpture fascinated him, and he'd wanted to see it close up ever since he'd arrived. He sent a quick text to Clayborne and made a plan to reconvene in the morning.

He shrugged off his suit jacket, removed his tie and loosened his shirt collar before rolling up the sleeves. Jago walked all the way to the sculpture and strolled around, craning his neck to get the full effect of its towering height. He sighed and checked his watch, then scanned the road behind him and spotted the sleek black limousine already waiting.

* * *

Meg pulled up in front of the house and hopped out of the car. Humming to herself, she ran inside and straight up to her room. She'd been dreaming of a refreshing dip in the swimming pool all day. The pool had been her mother's surprise birthday present to her husband on his sixtieth birthday. Betty Lou had decided not to waste her energy trying to persuade Gray that a pool was something all the family would enjoy, because he'd insist it was a needless extravagance. Instead she took him on vacation the week before his birthday, and the moment they left the installers arrived. By the time they returned from a week in Canada everything was done.

Meg hesitated before putting on her new scarlet-and-white polka-dot bikini. She'd sneaked out early and it was only four o'clock, meaning she should be safe from workaholic Jago turning up for at least another hour. Grabbing a towel, she ran back downstairs and straight outside.

'Well, I have to say the scenery suddenly improved.' Jago pushed himself out of the pool to sit on the side, dangling his long legs in the water. 'Come on in. The water's amazing.'

Water dripped down over his tanned skin and slicked-back his dark hair and emphasised his classic Italian good looks. *Remember how he treated you in Florence. Remember what he's doing to your business. Remember* . . . 'Are you playing hooky too?' she asked.

'Sort of.'

'I don't suppose you'd care to explain why you want to rip apart Mama Belle's and wipe out the best barbecue sauce in Nashville?' she said, putting him on the spot.

He stood up and rested his hand on her arm. His light touch sent shivers running through her. 'You're a smart woman. You must know the business is on the ropes. I'm surprised you got involved in the first place. I suppose Elliott talked you into it?' Jago's smile didn't reach his dark eyes. 'I suppose you turned into his fearsome guardian angel and swooped in to help him.'

'That's none of your business.'

'Oh but it definitely is, considering it interferes with my negotiations.' A teasing smile tugged at his generous mouth. 'Plus I have a personal stake here.'

'In what way?' she croaked.

'Don't play games, Meghan.' He dragged out her whole name. 'Does Elliott know about . . . us?'

'Us?' she squeaked. 'There is no *us*.'

'Really?'

'We went on one date last year and you stood me up on the second one. Elliott and I are old friends but that's it. There's no reason for me to tell him anything.'

'Are you completely oblivious to the fact the man's in love with you?'

'That's baloney.'

'Is it?' Jago asked in his quiet, straightforward way. 'I'll leave you to enjoy your swim.' He dropped his hand away and strolled over to where he'd left a large bright orange towel on one of the patio chairs. Meg watched him dry off and slip his large feet back into the black flip-flops he lived in when he wasn't dressed up for work.

The only thing Meg could think of doing was to jump right in the pool. The cool water briefly took her breath away, and by the time she'd swum a few frantic lengths she'd calmed down. Jago must be mad if he thought Elliott considered her as anything more than a good friend.

Are you sure, though? she asked herself. On more than a few occasions, her mother and aunt had hinted the same thing, but Meg had told them not to be silly. Surely none of them were right?

8

Jago reached the safety of his room and slammed the door shut behind him. He'd been enjoying a quiet swim until Meg arrived and planned to be out of the water long before she came home. Now he'd never look at red-and-white polka-dots the same way again.

Everything about Meg sparkled with life — it'd been the first thing that drew him to her, and it refused to leave him alone now. He needed to get out for the evening, because keeping up the facade of friendly indifference in front of Meg's parents was straining his acting abilities to the limit. There were a couple of bicycles out in the garage, and he'd been offered the use of them whenever he wanted. Franklin was only a couple of miles away, and going to check out the small town might be exactly what he needed.

Jago showered and got ready to leave. He'd have to tell the Harpers where he was going and crossed his fingers they wouldn't offer him Meg's company. On the way through the house, he spotted Gray sitting alone on the porch and took full advantage of the fact that the man never asked any unwanted questions. Five minutes later he was on his way.

He took the meandering back road Gray had recommended, and enjoyed seeing the countryside. This was horse country, and Jago cycled by several large farms he guessed were worth serious money. The sight of a 'For Sale' sign stuck in the ground by one gate made him stop. Jago balanced against the white picket fence and admired the solid wood building with its tall windows and gabled roof. There was nothing showy about the house, but he'd never been attracted to flash, preferring substance over glamour. Exactly like Meg. Jago glanced at his watch and shook his head. He'd managed a full fifteen minutes without thinking about her.

He forced himself to pull the bicycle upright and keep going. Maybe the largest, most decadent ice cream he could track down would cure what ailed him.

One massive death-by-chocolate sundae later, he admitted defeat. He ate his ice cream sitting outside one of the shops in the main street and did some people-watching. Apparently a lot of Civil War aficionados made their way here to check out all the sites connected with the Battle of Franklin. Swarms of people, mainly women dragging reluctant men along in their wake, checked out the shops and enjoyed the marginally cooler end to the day.

Every single minute, Jago wished Meg was with him. They could've had two spoons and shared the obscene amount of fudge brownies, four different types of ice cream, nuts, whipped cream and rich chocolate sauce he somehow managed to finish on his own. He dragged himself to his feet, surprised he could still move, then retrieved his bicycle from one of the racks scattered along the street and rode back towards the main road.

For some reason one of Elliott Docherty's stories took centre stage in his mind: 'Mama Belle's barbecue sauce was my grandmother's recipe, and back in the early twentieth century it was the first well-known sauce in the state of Tennessee. Nothing beat it. We could be that way again.'

Usually he came in and bought a business, split up the assets and sold them on without blinking. He made sure the workers got a decent payoff and that was it. But when he'd visited the factory, Jago had met people who were fourth-generation Mama Belle's workers and fiercely loyal to the company.

Out of interest he'd do a little investigating tonight and see what he came up with. If nothing else, it might stop him behaving like a lovesick teenage boy. Maybe.

* * *

'Do you know what's up with Jago?'

Meg focused on the onion she was dicing to avoid facing her mother. 'In what way?'

'He quit work early and looked real tired when he got back here. His swim didn't seem to do him much good either, and afterwards he went rushing off out like a cat with his tail on fire.' Betty Lou scoffed. 'Your Daddy's worse than useless too.'

'What's he done?' Meg set down the knife.

'He gave Jago directions into Franklin and let him go.' Disgust ran through her voice and Meg knew only too well what her mother meant. If her father was a 'normal' person, he'd have interrogated their guest and reported the answers back to his wife.

'Maybe he's tired from travelling and

struggling to get used to our hot, humid weather. I guess he simply wanted to get out and have a look around.'

'But why go on his own? Why didn't he ask you or any of us to come along?'

Because he wanted some peace and quiet? I know how he feels. Her mother would think that was crazy. Betty Lou was happiest surrounded by family and considered quiet time spent on her own as purgatory.

'I don't know, Mom.' Meg picked the knife back up. 'Is this enough onion?'

Betty Lou's eyes narrowed. 'Why are you changin' the subject?'

'I'm not. But I don't know the workings of Jago's mind any more than you do.' *Probably less.* 'Ask him later.'

'I can't do that. He'll think I'm nosey.'

Meg sighed. 'Then you'll have to give up and admit defeat.'

'I don't think much of that idea.' A smile tickled the corners of her mouth. 'You give up too easily, young lady.'

'What've you got in mind?'

'I'm not sure yet. I'll let you know. Hurry up with those mushrooms and peppers or Gray will be in here bangin' on the table and asking where his food is.'

They both knew that wasn't true, because he was the epitome of a patient man. He'd be on the porch reading the newspaper and drinking a beer while he waited to be told that supper was on the table. Whatever Meg's mother cooked would be wonderful in his eyes. He'd praise the food and the cook and offer to do the dishes afterwards. Meg wondered if her mother knew how lucky she was. *Yeah, she does.*

'Are you all right?'

Meg forced a bright smile, but her mother's continuing frown suggested she wasn't fooled. 'A bit tired, that's all.'

'Why don't *you* ask *him* out? That's the modern way, isn't it?'

'Ask who?'

'Jago, of course. I've watched you two circling each other and sending out interested signals ever since he arrived.'

Meg's cheeks flamed.

'I knew I was right.' Her mother's voice sang with unmistakeable triumph.

'I didn't say anything.'

'You don't need to, sweetheart. It's written all over your face.' She smirked. 'And his.'

'Don't be silly.'

'I happened to look out of the French windows when you went out to the pool this afternoon, and — '

'For goodness sake, it's like living in a fish bowl here.' Meg tossed the tea towel down on the countertop.

'Don't get in a huff. You must've seen the way he looked at you. I thought he was going to — '

'Stop right there.' Meg held up her hands. 'That's enough. I don't need you interfering with my private life — or at least what *should* be my private life if it was possible to have one.' Hurt radiated from her mother's bright blue eyes. 'I'm sorry. That didn't come out the way I intended.'

'Maybe not, but you meant it all the same. I'm not stupid. I'm aware you're nearly thirty and don't want to be back living at home again.' She touched Meg's arm. 'It's not what you pictured for yourself, is it?'

Meg couldn't see for the tears blinding her eyes and could only shake her head.

'Promise me you won't do something idiotic and run off to marry Elliott? He's a good guy and clearly loves you, but it'd be a disaster.'

'Marry Elliott? Are you out of your mind?'

Betty Lou raised her eyebrows and Meg didn't say another word.

'Fetch us a bottle of wine and pour two large glasses,' her mother said, returning to her usual brisk self. 'I'd better get this stir-fry started before your daddy dies of starvation.' A mischievous sparkle lit up her eyes. 'I'll say one more thing and shut up. Jago's a decent man with a sense of humour, and you could do a whole lot worse.

He's a good looker too, and I'd get some pretty grandbabies from the two of you.'

'Mother!' Meg complained. Tomorrow had to be an improvement over today, although she wouldn't place a bet on it the way things were going.

9

Jago's phone buzzed and he groped for it on the bedside table. He groaned as he listened to the message. It obviously didn't occur to his dear mother that the Harpers might not appreciate their house being turned into a hotel.

You'll never believe it, J, dear. I managed to talk Ernie into coming over there to visit you, and I picked up a couple of cheap tickets on the internet. We're at the airport now, and we'll be in Nashville tomorrow afternoon! Be a dear and sort things out with the Harpers. I'll ring you when we change planes in New York.

After a quick shower, Jago made his way down the hallway and heard voices in the kitchen. Gray gave him a friendly nod, but Meg kept her attention fixed on her plate. Betty Lou beamed at him as if he was a million-dollar lottery jackpot and she was the sole winner.

'Come sit down and I'll fix you a plate of breakfast. How does country ham, biscuits, scrambled eggs, fried apples and grits sound?'

'Um, wonderful, but I'm still full from last night. I ate ice cream for dinner. Lots of it.' Jago decided he'd better make an effort to be more sociable. 'I wouldn't turn down a cup of coffee if there's one going, though.'

'You can't turn down one of my biscuits, either.' She pointed to a tray of oversized golden-brown scones — at least, that was what they resembled to Jago. 'I'll tuck a small bite of country ham inside of one. You need something to keep you going 'til lunchtime.'

He gave in. 'How can I refuse? Thank you.' Jago sat down next to Gray and didn't rush into mentioning his mother's visit. He bided his time and answered all of Betty Lou's questions about how he'd spent his time in Franklin. When he described the decadent ice-cream sundae he'd demolished, Meg finally cracked a smile.

'You deserve to be the size of an elephant.'

There was no point putting off his request any longer. Jago knew he was being stupid because the Harpers would welcome his parents with open arms, but their visit added another layer of complication he didn't need. As soon as the words left his mouth, Betty Lou jumped up and flung her arms around him.

'Well, isn't that the best news. I can't wait to meet your mama. I didn't think we'd ever see Ernie again unless I managed to drag this one out of Tennessee.' She pointed at Gray. 'You be sure to tell your folks they can stay as long as they like.'

Jago managed a gracious smile and thanked her. 'If you'll excuse me, I need to get my things together. My driver will be here soon.'

'Off you go. Wherever it is you're going,' Betty Lou probed. 'Meg's cooking the only thing she knows how to fix this evening for supper — barbecued short ribs. Be here at six.'

Jago knew a command when he heard one.

* * *

Meg hadn't been stupid enough to tell her mother about the motive behind her offer to cook that night. She'd revamped the Mama Belle's label and printed off a few samples. *Do you really think you're going to convince Jago to save the business with a plate of ribs?* They were running out of time, because Elliott had admitted yesterday that his fundraising plans weren't going well.

She'd given her mother detailed instructions about getting the ribs started, but needed to get back home in good time to work her magic. Meg usually made her own sauce, but tonight she planned to use Mama Belle's instead.

After locking her office, she headed off down the street to the car park. She turned on the engine but nothing happened, and when she called the rescue service they said it would take them an hour to arrive. Jago was her only hope, so she sent him a quick text.

Am I interrupting your work?

He replied instantly. *No. What I can do for you, apart from hopping on the next plane back to England?*

Very funny. Are you going back to Red Roof soon?

I am.

Meg swallowed her pride. *Could I hitch a lift? My car's broken down.*

Not a problem. Give me ten minutes.

I'll walk back to the office.

No, we'll pick you up at your car. Fewer possible questions that way.

Thank goodness he retained some common sense, even if hers had flown out of the window.

★   ★   ★

Jago left the building with a few blunt words to the board: 'Present your counter-offer first thing Monday morning, or I'll give you my final figures and forty-eight hours to decide.'

'Ready, Mr. Merryn?' Ron stood by the car waiting for him.

Jago got his act together. 'Yes, thank you. We need to drive over to the Peabody Street car park and pick up Ms. Harper. Her car's broken down, so we'll take her back with us to Franklin.'

'No problem, sir.'

He climbed into the front passenger seat next to Ron, and the chauffeur raised his eyes but didn't make any comment. Normally Jago spread out in the back, but he didn't want to crowd Meg and make her feel awkward. When they tracked her down, Ron got out and opened the rear door.

'Is someone coming to see to your car?' Jago asked.

'Yep. They'll be here in an hour or so. I really appreciate the lift.'

'No problem. I'm not going out of

my way, am I?' he teased. 'No way was I going to miss your culinary master-piece.'

'I'm sorry my mom dragooned you into coming.'

'Are you?' Jago wished she'd be honest with him, but Meg stared out of the window and didn't reply. At least she didn't lie, and for some absurd reason that gave him hope. *Do you seriously think she'll give you another chance?*

During the quiet drive, Ron occasionally glanced over at Jago and then at Meg in his rear-view mirror. Jago had no doubt that most drivers had a few good stories up their sleeve about their passengers, and he wondered what Ron might say about them.

'Everybody out,' Ron joked, and he stopped outside the front door. 'Do you need me tomorrow, sir?'

Clayborne Williams had talked him into playing a round of golf and meeting some of his Nashville business cronies. He'd boasted about his membership at the city's most prestigious course, and it'd taken all Jago's restraint to refrain from saying that if the other man devoted more energy to his business, he might not be in danger of losing it. Jago found golf tedious, but he'd learned to play adequately for the same reason he'd learned the correct way to eat an artichoke — to enhance his business dealings and not embarrass himself.

'I need to be in town by ten, so how about we go for around quarter past nine? Ms. Harper could ride in with us if she needs to go anywhere.'

'Please don't concern yourself about me. If I need to go somewhere and don't have my own car back, I'll borrow my father's truck.'

Behind her back, Ron drew a finger across his throat and Jago stifled a grin.

'Fair enough.' He jumped out of the car first this time and opened her door. 'Off you go and work magic on those ribs.'

She stiffly thanked them both and strode off into the house.

'Quite something, isn't she?' Ron chuckled. 'Reminds me of my wife. Feisty and darn pretty with it. Are you two . . . you know?'

'Not exactly. We almost were once.'

'Thought so.' Ron shook his head. 'Women mess up your head, don't they?'

'Certainly do. You've been married for ages. Any advice?' Over the last week they'd swapped stories while travelling back and forth to Nashville. The driver wasn't much older than Jago, but he'd married straight out of high school, and his wife and five daughters had him wrapped around their little fingers.

'My Emmaline was similar to your young lady when we met, and determined not to give in. Made me work for every single minute she granted me, and they were few and far between to start with.'

'How'd you win her over?'

Ron burst into uncontrolled laughter. 'Heck, I'm still working on it.' He wagged his finger. 'That's the secret.'

'I don't get it.'

'You will.'

'Thanks.' Jago told his driver about tonight's planned dinner and a broad grin creased Ron's face.

'The mother's out to get you. Bit like in the old days when they made the girls play the piano to impress a man or show them their watercolours.' Ron's cheeks flushed. 'My other half watches those Jane Austen things on public television. She says it's because of the clever dialogue, but I think it's the men wearing tight pants and riding horses everywhere.'

Jago suspected Ron was right about Meg's mother. If Meg thought anyone was trying to steer her into Jago's arms, she'd run a mile in the opposite direction.

'Good luck, sir. I'd better be off. Homemade fried chicken tonight, and if I'm late it'll be a long night sleeping on the couch.'

Jago opened his wallet and peeled off

several twenty-dollar bills. 'Buy your lovely wife some flowers.' Ron tried to protest but he pressed them into his hand. 'Tell her you've been doing your agony uncle bit. You've given me a lot to think about. I might thank you later, or not. We'll see.'

'Thanks, and best of luck, sir.' Ron drove off and Jago waited until the car disappeared before walking towards the house.

Heck, I'm still working on it. That's the secret.

A light bulb went off in Jago's head. Obviously his plans needed to be adjusted where Meg was concerned. If she could stop seeing him as the enemy, they might get somewhere, but the problem was trust. And what exactly would Jago do next if she ever did start to trust him?

10

Meg brushed the thick sauce over the ribs, ready to take them outside to finish cooking on the grill. That morning she'd rubbed them with her own spice mixture before letting them sit in the fridge all day, and given her mother strict instructions to roast the ribs for two hours in the afternoon to get the cooking process started.

If Jago weren't joining them, she could relax and enjoy herself. Being in the same car with him had tested her resolve quite enough. He was just so . . . *there*, filling up the space with his dark eyes and teasing smile.

'Something's smelling good. Anything I can do to help?' Jago asked as he strolled into the kitchen. He selected a banana from the dish and peeled it back to take a big bite before giving Meg a sheepish grin. 'Sorry. I skipped lunch and I'm starved.'

'No problem. I'm going to finish the ribs off on the grill. Why don't you join my dad on the porch? It'll be another half-hour or so before it's all ready.'

'Thanks, but I'd prefer to stay here if you don't mind.'

His frank reply took her breath away. She clasped the tray of meat, not willing to be let down by her unsteady hands and risk dropping the whole lot on the floor. 'Whatever.' She turned her back on him and walked towards the door, but he put the half-eaten banana on the table and beat her to it.

'I know the work thing is between us and that I didn't treat you right in Florence. I totally get that you're testing me, and I don't blame you. I intend to prove myself to you one way or the other.' He lifted his left hand to caress her face, rubbing his thumb in slow circles over her hot skin. Meg struggled to breathe as he lowered his mouth to hers, but at the last second he turned and brushed his lips over her cheek. Regret burned in his eyes as he drew back.

'You'd better get busy cooking the ribs instead of my brain.'

Meg wished she was the sort of woman who made men forget all logic and sense.

'It's not down to any lack of desire on my part. Trust me.' His wry smile touched her. 'Trust is the root of the problem. You don't trust me, and when we can get past that we might stand a chance.'

'A chance of what?'

'I don't know, Meghan. I wish . . . '

'What?'

Over Meg's shoulder he spotted Betty Lou bustling into the kitchen and stepped to one side. 'I wish you'd hurry up and get that meat cooked. I'm starving, and I'll eat it raw in a minute.' Confusion flared in her soft gray eyes and he gestured behind them. A good-humoured smile warmed her face, and he sensed her gratitude for saving them both from looking foolish in front of her shrewd mother.

'Sorry.' Meg laughed. 'Won't be long.'

'I came to check on the potatoes,' Betty Lou declared. 'Go with her, son. I'm sure she can do with a hand.'

'I'm happy to help if you need me, but otherwise I'll join your father.' *In other words, it's your choice.* Her shoulders relaxed and he knew he'd said the right thing.

'I'm okay. Go and talk man stuff.'

'Will do. What are the approved topics of conversation? Sports, women and beer?'

'You got it.' Meg winked and breezed on out of the door.

Betty Lou gave him a searching stare. 'What's going on with you two?'

Wouldn't you like to know.

'There's something I can't put my finger on.'

I bet that doesn't happen often.

'My sister Sarah said something odd the day you arrived.'

Jago kept a pleasant smile on his face.

87

'She got the impression you and Meg had met before. I told her it was impossible, but now I'm not so sure.' She hesitated, but Jago held his tongue. 'If you're going to stand there with your mouth taped shut, I can be patient.'

'Patient' was the very last word he'd use to describe Meg's mother. 'If you'll excuse me, I'll grab a couple of beers and go shoot the breeze with Gray. I haven't seen him all day.' He raided the fridge and made it all the way out into the hall before she yelled after him.

'I'll find out, you know. One way or another.'

Jago ignored her and headed for the porch.

'Kicked you out of the kitchen, have they?'

'Yes. Thank goodness.' He laughed and dropped down into the nearest rocking chair. 'Here you go. Don't know about you, but I need this.'

'Had a long day?'

'You could say that.' Jago hated not being honest about the real reason he was in Nashville and came to a swift decision. Meg would just have to tolerate her family knowing, and maybe she'd see it as his attempt to help. Jago quietly told Gray about his bid to take over and break up the barbecue sauce business.

'That all makes sense now. I knew something was up, though Meg kept denying it. I wasn't a fan of giving up her good job in Knoxville and putting her money into Mama Belle's in the first place. The problem is, she and Elliott are like this.' He crossed his fingers. 'He needed help and she gave it — same as she's done since they were kids.'

'Apart from the few younger directors, they're an old entrenched business and not looking to change. I'm sorry. She'll be mad when she finds out I've talked to you, but it's been eating away at me to say nothing.'

'I respect that.' Gray's eyes twinkled. 'I suppose you've met the Docherty boy.' He took a long swallow of his beer and wiped his mouth.

'Yes.'

'He's not a bad guy. Loves Meg of course, but he's not right for her.'

'Do you think she sees that?'

'That he's not right, or that he loves her?'

'Either. Both.'

Gray turned serious. 'Not sure we should be talking this way. It could come under the heading of disloyal.'

'Fair enough.' Jago changed tack. 'Completely off-the-wall question — is Mama Belle's sauce any good?'

'Yeah. My mother never bought anything else, but it went out of fashion.'

'Thanks. You've given me something to think about. By the way, I'm playing golf with Clayborne Williams tomorrow, although not by choice.'

'Rather you than me.' Gray chuckled. 'Betty Lou's always pointing him out in the paper at some fancy party. Williams and all the old guys have coasted along for years. I'm not surprised the business is run into the ground. Meg's tried her best, but she's wasting her talents there.'

Jago finished his beer and crushed the can in his hand. 'I usually come in, do a deal and leave.'

'Not as straightforward this time?'

He shrugged. 'Maybe. I'm not sure.'

'I don't know anything about big business, but I'm guessing it's not that different from dealing with cows,' Gray mused. 'Sometimes one gets to you. Can't put your finger on it but it does.'

'You're right. The people at the factory did that. Some of them are fourth-generation workers and it's all they know.' Jago tried to smile. 'They're so damn proud of the sauce. You'd think it was gold dust.'

'You haven't got kids, have you?'

He shook his head, wondering what that had to do with anything.

'You hate to hear anyone speak out against them, no matter what they've done. Same as those guys with the sauce. They're not dumb. They know the business is struggling. But they still don't want some smart-mouthed Brit coming in and telling them where to go.' Gray laughed. 'I guess you know what I mean.'

Jago grinned. 'No offence taken.'

'Have you ever saved a business before?'

He shook his head.

'There's a first time for everything.' Gray's laconic comment struck deep. 'Think about it.'

'I will. Thanks.'

'Happy to help.' Gray patted his stomach. 'I wish the women would hurry up with the food.' Tactfully he closed the subject.

'Me too.'

Betty Lou appeared at the door and glanced between the two of them. 'What're you pair up to? Supper's ready.'

Gray jumped up and hugged his wife. 'Nothing, hon. Just drinking and talking about this and that.'

She pulled away from him. 'Grayson

Cody Harper, you'll tell me the truth in bed tonight.' Now she included Jago in her fierce glare. 'Or you'll both regret it. Trust me.' Betty Lou stalked off, and the two men could only look at each other and shrug. They'd no doubt she was right.

11

Meg couldn't stop smiling. The ribs were the best she'd ever made, and Jago ate more than anyone.

'You did a good job. They tasted different tonight. Did you tweak the recipe?' Her mother's innocent question gave Meg the perfect lead-in.

'Sort of. The sauce is new — well, not exactly new. For a change I didn't make my own today.' She reached behind her to where she'd hidden the bottle behind the iced-tea pitcher. 'I thought I'd give Mama Belle's a try.' Meg set the bottle with its newly designed label in front of Jago. 'Did you like it?'

A sliver of annoyance flitted across his face. 'It's good. Smoky and sweet at the same time.' He picked up the bottle and studied the label, running his fingers over the vintage-style font she'd chosen and the picture of Mama Belle she'd discovered in an old Nashville newspaper.

Gray had guessed she was up to something. 'I don't know about y'all, but I'm ready for coffee. You'd better hold dessert. I'm stuffed.'

'If you're going to do that, I think I'll go for a walk.' Jago pushed his chair back from the table. 'Would you care to join me, Meg? I know you've been stuck inside all day too.'

'I need to clear up all this.' She gestured around the untidy kitchen.

'Don't worry about that, hon. Your daddy and I will see to it. You go and get some fresh air.'

It's July. It's Tennessee. We won't enjoy fresh air again until October. Meg recognised the implacable look on her mother's face and didn't have the energy to fight back. 'Okay. I'll go and change out of my flip-flops.'

'Good idea.' Jago's deep brown eyes rested on her.

Meg plastered on a smile and fled the kitchen.

'If you'll excuse me.' Jago made his escape before Betty Lou could ask more awkward questions. He hurried back to his room and changed into his trainers before going in search of his walking companion.

He waited in the hall until she came back downstairs, and couldn't help noticing that she'd changed into a pair of flattering red shorts. 'Ready?'

'As ready as I'll ever be.' Meg headed towards the front door. 'Where do you want to go on this famous walk?'

Jago tossed the ball in her court. 'Take me to your favourite place on the property.'

'Fine.'

'Lead the way.'

Meg stalked off down the path leading around the back of the house, and for the next quarter of an hour they didn't speak, only walked. She made her way along the perimeter fence before branching off and hiking up a steep gravel path alongside a stand of old gnarled trees. Jago easily kept up with her, but the humidity took its toll and he wasn't sorry when Meg stopped in the shade of one large oak. She wiped the sweat off her forehead with the back of her hand and half-smiled when he did the same.

Meg pointed towards a small wooden structure on the crest of the hill. 'That's the original cabin my great-great-grandfather built in 1860. Do you want to take a look inside?'

'That'd be great.'

Meg couldn't hide her enthusiasm as she showed him around. Every log of wood and rough-hewn window frame came to life through her lyrical descriptions, and he didn't want her to stop.

Her awkwardness flooded back. 'Sorry, I got carried away. Elliott always says I could bore for Tennessee about this place.'

'I'd have thought he'd be interested in the local history.'

'If you'd seen the Docherty place, you'd know why he isn't overly impressed by this.' She laughed. 'This farm is miniscule compared to the land he'll inherit one day, including a house that resembles Tara on steroids.'

Jago laughed out loud, and when Meg joined in he ached to pull her into his arms and kiss her until all the nonsense between them faded away. Then reality slammed back. 'Why did you pull that trick with the barbecue sauce tonight?'

Meg turned away to stare out of the window, and Jago crossed the room to stand behind her. He planted his hands on her shoulders and eased her around to face him. 'Why, Meg?'

'I want you to see that the business isn't some abstract thing. It's good and it's worth saving. Don't you ever wonder about the people whose businesses you tear apart and what happens to them after you leave?'

'By the time I step in it's too late for most of them. You told me about the struggles you've had over the last year at Mama Belle's, and that my money will leave the older directors free to retire with dignity or move on somewhere else in the case of you and a few others.'

'But what happens to the workers? Manufacturing jobs are hard to come by these days.'

'Face facts, Meg — the business is one step away from bankruptcy. They'll lose their jobs anyway. I'm running a business, not a charity. My shareholders expect decent dividends at the end of the year, and it's my place to give it to them.'

'I'm really trying to understand. Help me.'

'It's complicated.'

'I'm not stupid. I can understand words of more than two syllables.'

Jago sighed. 'I didn't mean it that way. I always seem to say the wrong thing with you.'

'You didn't in Florence,' Meg ventured. 'At least, Lucca Raffaele didn't.'

He slid his arms around her waist. 'He's the better side of me. The easygoing man who's not always worried about what might happen tomorrow and that it'll leave him struggling to pay next month's bills.'

'Was your childhood hard?'

'Hard? It depends how you define the word. Did I have a home, food to eat, and clothes to wear? Yes, never an issue. But did I hide under the bedclothes to avoid hearing another blazing row? Or come home from school with a knot in my stomach wondering if my dad would be there that day or if he'd gone again? Definitely. When he left for good when I was sixteen, my mum needed me to step up, and I did.' Jago hurried to put a stop to the pity written all over Meg's face. 'I'm not looking for sympathy.'

'I know, but I can't help feeling for you.'

Jago stepped away and shoved his hands deep in his pockets. 'It could've been worse.'

'Yeah, but it could've been a lot better too.'

'Not everyone gets your fairytale upbringing.'

What right did he have to sum up her family in a few trite words? 'Every fairytale has its dark side,' she said.

'What're you getting at?'

'Nothing as harsh as your experiences, but there are personal things my parents don't talk about with strangers and wouldn't appreciate me sharing with you.'

'Is that what we are — strangers?'

'I thought I had an inkling about Lucca Raffaele, but you I don't have a clue about. Are you going to prove me wrong?'

Meg had caught him off guard. 'Probably not.' He pulled himself together. 'Your mother's apple pie is calling me. Let's walk on back.'

'Okay. I know where I stand now.'

'Do you?'

'Yes. I'm ready for apple pie too.' She strode away and didn't wait to see if he followed.

Jago let her go. Lucca would've swept

her into his arms, made her laugh, and smothered her with kisses until they both forgot whatever nonsense they'd disagreed about. But Jago wasn't that man. People who allowed their hearts to rule their heads turned into men like his father — irresponsible, volatile and unreliable, always following the latest pipe dream and leaving a trail of unhappiness in their wake. When Marco Raffaele finally stayed away for good, Jago's relief was indescribable. He hadn't seen or heard from his father in nearly twenty years, which was fine with him.

If he had any sense, he'd get on the next plane to London and send his deputy in to wrap up the deal. *So, what's keeping you? A five-foot-eight brunette with smoky gray eyes who makes killer barbecue ribs?* Thank goodness his mother and Ernie were arriving tomorrow, which would take the attention off him.

He took his time wandering back to the house and sneaked in the back door to his rooms. As far as the Harpers were concerned, he'd gone to bed and wasn't interested in coffee, pie or any more conversation. Meg could concoct whatever story she liked to explain his absence.

Fifteen minutes later someone banged on his door, but Jago didn't move. Gray called his name a few times, asked if he was okay and knocked once more. 'Betty Lou sent me. I'm supposed to tell you that if you get hungry later, there'll be leftover pie in the fridge.'

'Thanks,' Jago broke his silence.

'No problem. Goodnight.'

Jago stripped off his clothes and headed for the shower. The pounding water would clean his sticky skin but it wouldn't wash away Meghan Harper. *Do you want it to?* He roughly towelled himself dry and pulled on a clean pair of boxers and a T-shirt before stretching out on the bed. With the pillows plumped up behind his head, he opened his laptop.

He'd seen enough bottles of Mama Belle's sauce at the factory to recognise the difference in the one Meg had showed off earlier. The original label was dull, but Meg's new design had the quasi-vintage look people fell for these days. Ideas jumbled around in his head, and he started to make notes in an effort to sort them out.

Have you ever saved a business before? There's a first time for everything. Think on it.

He forgot all notion of time and let his mind run free. Without the usual constraints, the ideas flowed, and a surge of excitement he hadn't experienced in years spiralled through him.

12

'How come you upset the boy?' Betty Lou persisted.

Meg carried on pouring herself a mug of coffee, adding a splash of cream and sugar. 'I'm tired. I'm going to read for a while. I'll see you in the morning.' She caught her father's sympathetic glance but walked out of the kitchen without another word. Meg knew she couldn't play the part of warm, friendly hostess when Jago's mother and stepfather arrived tomorrow.

Her old college friend had nagged Meg for ages to visit her in Chattanooga, and she'd made the excuse of having too much work, although the truth lay somewhere between that and a nasty touch of envy. Lola, with her devoted husband Jack, two adorable children and successful online crafting business, was living Meg's dream life.

Before she could have second thoughts, Meg rang Lola, and her friend's shrieks of joy came close to bursting her eardrum.

'We'll have so much fun! Jack can watch the boys while we enjoy a little girl-time. We'll shop and gossip and drink cocktails. I want to hear all about your exciting life. It's gotta be more fun than changing diapers and cleaning peanut butter out of my hair.'

Meg's heart sank. *At least you'll be away from Red Roof Farm and Jago.* 'I'll be there by lunchtime tomorrow.' She didn't want to tell her mother about her plans, so she'd sneak out early and leave a note. If she timed it right, her father would still be out helping with the morning milking. They didn't have many cows these days, and after Gray's slight stroke a couple of years ago the doctor and her mother persuaded him to semi-retire. These days he did as much or as little as he felt like.

She showered before getting ready

for bed to make it easier to slip away unnoticed in the morning. Meg threw a few clothes in a small bag and at the last minute added a black cocktail dress and heels in case Lola wanted to hit the town. She crawled into bed and set her alarm before closing her eyes and trying to sleep.

After she'd come back from Florence, it'd been a long time before Lucca Raffaele didn't haunt her dreams. There'd been something indefinably special about their date — at least she'd thought so, until he didn't turn up the next night. Now he was lodged in her head again, prodding and teasing her to notice him.

She'd give herself a reprieve until Monday and hope the break helped.

* * *

'Going somewhere?'

The sight of Jago lounging against the kitchen door startled Meg. Her equilibrium wasn't helped by the fact that he only wore thin black sport shorts and a matching sleeveless T-shirt with his running shoes. It didn't make sense that Jago's messy dark hair and unshaven face only made him more attractive.

'Ouch.' Hot tea splashed over her hand because she hadn't fitted the top on her travel mug properly. 'Will you please stop doing that?' He lifted one dark eyebrow but didn't speak. 'Are you spying on me?'

'I'm going for a run.' He patted his flat stomach. 'Got to do something to counteract all the barbecued ribs I ate last night and the mountains of food your mother's been shovelling into me.' Jago dragged his gaze down over her. 'So *are* you going somewhere?'

Meg pointed to the envelope on the table. 'I've left that for my parents. They'll understand.'

'And I wouldn't?'

She sighed and gave an abbreviated version of the truth, making it sound as though she'd planned this trip for a while. 'Now may I go?'

'I didn't take you for a coward.' The blunt statement sucked her breath away. 'Lots of other things, yes. Smart. Beautiful. Funny. Hard-working. Loving.' A quirky smile pulled at his generous mouth.

'How dare you! If anyone's a coward, it's you.' Meg checked the clock on the wall. 'I'm going.' She abandoned her mug on the table. 'I'll see you on Monday.' Opening the door, she crashed straight into her father, who held out his hands to stop her from tripping over.

'Meg! Where are — '

She cut her father off mid-sentence and pointed at Jago. 'Ask him. He knows *everything*.'

Both men stared at each other, then back at Meg, but she stalked off without another word.

'Feisty girl, isn't she?' Gray's laconic comment drew a smile out of Jago. 'Any coffee going?'

'I was about to make myself some. I'll get it.'

'You're a terrible liar, son.' He limped into the room and pulled out a stool to sit down on. 'I may be stubborn but I'm not an idiot. I know I've overdone it this morning, so I'll thank you and accept your offer.'

Meg's father rose even higher in Jago's estimation. Anyone who could admit they needed help was courageous in his book.

If anyone's the coward, it's you.

'Is something wrong?'

Jago came perilously close to blurting out the truth. Although he realised not everybody's marriages and relationships failed, the idea of taking a chance and getting it wrong scared him. He wished he had the nerve to ask Gray's honest opinion, but in the end the older man was Meg's father. Gray would defend and protect his daughter because that was what good parents did.

He pushed the envelope across the

table. 'Nope, just tired. Is instant coffee okay?'

'Sure.'

While the water boiled, Jago checked back over his shoulder to see Gray take out a pair of reading glasses from his shirt pocket and slip them on. 'She's gone to visit her old college girlfriend in Chattanooga.'

'It'll do her good to have a break.'

'Yep, it sure will. By the way, Betty Lou knows.'

'Knows what?' Jago asked.

'About the problems at Mama Belle's. She wheedled it out of me last night.' Gray frowned. 'What did you *think* I was talking about?'

Jago carried their drinks over to the table. 'There you go.'

'Thanks.' Gray took a sip. 'You didn't answer my question.'

'No, I didn't, because I'm not sure how.'

'I don't want to see Meg get hurt.'

'I understand that.'

'So?' Gray wasn't letting this go.

'It's not straightforward.'

'Nothing ever is.'

'Meg wouldn't appreciate me saying too much.'

'I don't care. You told me about the business troubles and that she could lose her money and her job. What else is going on? I can't help if I don't know the problem.' Gray fixed Jago with a penetrating stare. 'If the problem is *you*, then you can leave, family or not.'

'Fair enough.' Jago stood up and took the remains of his coffee over to dump in the sink. He rinsed out the mug and set it on the draining board.

'Where're you going?'

'To pack. My driver is coming soon and he can take me to a hotel in Nashville. I'll stay there until my business is wrapped up.' He'd sweep away the idiotic notion of saving Mama Belle's. 'I'll tell my mother and Ernie that I moved because it's more convenient for my work — that's not a total lie.'

'There's no need to take it that far. I didn't — '

'Don't. Please.' Jago held up his hand. 'I understand your position, and I'd feel the same if it was my daughter.'

'But what am I goin' to say to Betty Lou?' A touch of panic laced Gray's voice. 'She won't believe some damn fool story about it being 'more convenient'.'

Jago heard footsteps and glanced over to the door. *I'd better think of something quick or we're both screwed.*

13

With the miles disappearing behind her, Meg's shoulders lost the painful, tense knots that'd taken up residence since Jago had walked back into her life. Calling him by that name still seemed wrong, because in her heart he'd always be Lucca.

Stop thinking about him.

She'd come to the conclusion that if she couldn't have what her folks shared, she preferred to remain single. Since her last failed dating attempts, she'd made the decision never to stay with any man who didn't make life better simply by being there, share her quirky sense of humour, and set her pulse racing.

Like Jago, you mean?

She'd got back to him again. Meg cranked up the radio and determinedly sang along to her favourite country music station. The outskirts of Chattanooga crept up on her and she concentrated on finding Lola's house.

The neighbourhood, with its cookie-cutter homes, manicured lawns and two-car garages, was the opposite of everything they'd dreamed of in their college days. They'd intended to live somewhere artistic and edgy — one week New York topped the list, and the next it'd be San Francisco or Austin, Texas. That was before Lola got back together with Jack, her high-school sweetheart, and married him the Saturday after graduation. Lola moved to Chattanooga, where Jack was a banker, and Meg took the first public relations job she was offered and stayed in Knoxville. She'd never really settled into the corporate culture of a large business and missed her family, Red Roof Farm and everything connected with life in a small town. Elliott's offer came at the perfect time — at least she'd thought so until she realised what she'd got herself into.

Meg rested her hands on the steering wheel and took a few deep, steadying breaths before getting out. The front door burst open and Lola rushed towards her with two small children running along behind. The tow-headed boy made a desperate grab for his mother's shorts, but Jack bounded out from the house and caught hold of him. He flashed Meg a bright apologetic smile and swept his son up in his arms before taking hold of the little girl's hand too.

'I'll take the monsters back in. Good to see you, Meg.'

'Sorry about the welcome party,' Lola joked. 'Come here. It's been too long.' They clung to each other in a tight hug and Meg fought back tears. 'What's up?'

'Nothing.'

'Yes there is. Don't lie.'

Meg sighed. 'It's — '

'Don't tell me. Complicated. You always were complicated. A man. It has to be a man.' Her hazel eyes narrowed. 'Please don't tell me Elliott's finally convinced you he's the one?'

'God, Lola, not you too! Elliott's a friend. He always has been. Nothing more. Nothing less. End of story.'

Lola rolled her eyes. 'Yeah, right. We'll talk about that later. Jack's taking the kids over to his mother's this afternoon and not bringing them back until after she's fed them all dinner.' Her brilliant smile resurfaced. 'By then we'll be glammed up and out on the town.'

'Oh, okay.'

'Don't sound too enthusiastic.'

Meg tried to see this weekend from her friend's point of view. Lola obviously loved being with her children, but it wasn't always easy and must have its frustrations. 'Sorry. We'll have fun. I promise.'

'Next time try saying that with a smile instead of a grimace.'

'I will.' Meg's over-the-top enthusiasm made them both laugh. 'Let me get my bags and you can give me the guided tour.'

Lola's eyes sparkled. 'I know it's more *Stepford Wives* than artsy, but . . . it's home. I found out none of the other stuff matters.'

'You're very lucky.' The words slipped out and Meg wished they didn't sound resentful. 'I didn't mean — '

'I know. But you're right. I *am* lucky, and I'm thankful every single day.'

'So many people aren't.' Meg suspected she wasn't as grateful as she should be for what she did have.

Lola nodded. 'Come on. We'll talk more later. I figure we'll play with the little ones for a couple of hours while Jack gets his strength up for the rest of the day. It'll be our penance for all the cocktails we'll indulge in tonight.'

'Perfect.' At this moment, simply to be away from Red Roof Farm and everything connected to it made this a good day for Meg.

★ ★ ★

'Stay there and don't say a word.' Betty Lou glared at Gray and he slumped back on the stool. '*You* can talk.' She poked Jago's arm. 'This useless husband of mine told me all about the Mama Belle's tangle last night. Telling lies always catches up with you.'

'I didn't lie,' Jago protested.

'Didn't tell the truth either, did you?' Betty Lou skewered him. 'All that confidential business nonsense. We're family. If you'd said what you'd come here for, you wouldn't have caught Meg out that first day, would you? Poor girl.'

Meg hadn't been the only shocked one, but Jago wasn't stupid enough to say so. 'You're right.' He caught Gray's amused expression.

'She gave up a decent job to come back here and she's put everything into it. Is she going to lose it all?' Betty Lou demanded.

Put on the spot, he wasn't sure how to respond. 'Ask me again after Monday. Elliott and a few of the others are trying to put together a counter-bid.' Jago shrugged. 'Right now it doesn't look likely they'll succeed, but it's possible. Whatever happens, there will be payouts for all the investors. She won't be bankrupted.'

'What about Gray's idea? You going to give it a try?'

This was why business and family shouldn't mix. They knew nothing of what it took to reinvigorate a business, and Jago wasn't about to go into long tedious explanations. 'I've got to give it some thought.'

'You're telling me to keep my nose out, aren't you?'

He couldn't resist a brief smile. 'Pretty much.' Jago waited for the explosion, but surprisingly Betty Lou went quiet. It didn't last long.

'So what was this one talkin' about when I came in?' She pointed at Gray. 'I caught a mention of something I wouldn't believe. Try me.'

'I overreacted and spoke a bit hastily,' Gray replied before Jago had the chance to come up with a reasonable explanation for his planned move. 'Don't throw a fit, honey, but Jago's moving into a hotel downtown for a couple of reasons.' He kept talking over his wife's attempt to protest. 'It's more convenient and puts a distance between himself and Meg — for work reasons.'

Betty Lou's eyes narrowed. 'Nothing to do with the way they're eyeing each other up all the time? I told her to ask him out, but she's a stubborn girl.'

A hot flush raced up Jago's neck, and he wished he could crawl under the kitchen table and stay there.

'You shouldn't have done that,' Gray reprimanded his wife. 'They're adults. It's none of our business.'

'Of course it is,' she fired back at him. 'We'll see what Cecily and Ernie have to say about this tomorrow.'

Jago almost said it wasn't any of their business either, but Gray's warning glance shut him up.

'Is he serious? You're really going?' Betty Lou asked.

'Yes; it's for the best. You've been very kind to have me to stay.'

'I expect you back here at six tomorrow for a family party to welcome your folks. No excuses.'

Jago could hardly refuse the three-line whip, and her satisfied smile told him she knew it. 'I'll look forward to it very much.'

'Do you want me to pick them up from the airport in the afternoon?' Gray offered.

'That'd be great. Thanks.'

'No problem.'

'I'd better go and get my things together. Ron will be here with the car soon.' Jago hurried from the kitchen before Betty Lou could prolong things any further. So much for a straightforward, uncomplicated business deal mixed with a brief family visit. He wasn't going to forget Nashville in a hurry. Or Meg. His heart told him he'd never forget her no matter how hard he tried. Years ago he'd laid down strict rules for himself where long-term commitment was concerned. Until he met Meg, it hadn't been difficult to stick to his rules; but after only one date she'd tempted him to break them, and he was getting increasingly close to doing the same again. This move was the only way out, and he hoped it would work because he didn't have a clue what else to do.

14

Josh changed into in his golfing clothes and prepared to waste a few hours. His first boss had taught him a whole lot of important things unconnected with business, and the power of a half-decent golf game was one of them. Good manners and dressing appropriately were two of the others. For a young man from a less privileged background, the entry-level job in London opened up possibilities he never knew existed, and from then on he'd never looked back. Sam Wetherspoon had taught him the rules in order that Jago could choose whether or not to break them.

His phone beeped with a text from Ron to say he'd arrived with the car. By the middle of next week he'd to be back in London and grateful for a lucky escape.

Liar.

Meg hit the nail on the head when she asked if he had a home to go back to. He owned multiple properties around the world, but they were nothing more than real-estate investment deals. Before he could sink into more self-pity, he gathered up his belongings and opened the bedroom door.

Gray was walking down the hall towards him. 'I thought you might like a hand.'

'Thanks.' Jago passed over his computer bag. 'I can manage the rest.'

'Travelling light. I remember.'

He forced out a laugh. 'It's the only way.'

'In some things.'

They both knew what he was referring to, and Jago wasn't getting into *that* discussion. He picked up the rest of his luggage. 'I'll give you a ring later and let you know my room number at the hotel.' They headed out together towards the front of the house.

'Good morning, Mr. Merryn.' Ron

always kept up appearances in front of other people, but once they were in the car everything changed. They'd become friends, and the man wasn't afraid to tell Jago what he thought. 'Renaissance Hotel, right?' The touch of sarcasm didn't escape Jago's notice. When he'd called Ron to inform him about his new plans, the driver had bent his ear about why he wanted to make such a stupid move. Ron had fallen under Meg's spell the day they'd brought her home, and declared her to be Jago's soulmate, as if such a thing existed outside of fairytales.

'Yes, thank you, Ron.' Jago didn't rise to the bait. He shook hands with Gray and climbed into the front passenger seat. Usually he looked forward to the drive and never minded if they got stuck in traffic, because it gave them the chance to talk for longer, but today not so much.

It didn't take Ron long to start in on him. 'I hoped the Harpers would've convinced you not to be dumb.'

'Don't hold back or anything,' Jago retorted. 'I could put in a complaint and get you fired.'

Ron chuckled. 'Nah, you won't. You're an honest man and don't get much of that in your line of work. I'm a refreshing change.'

'That's a word for you.'

'I'm guessing you didn't have breakfast. You want to do a drive-thru before you go to your fancy golf club?' Ron used Jago's weakness for a certain fast food chain's sausage-egg muffins as an unsubtle form of blackmail.

'That'd be great. We're lunching at the club after I've lost.'

'I can't imagine you losing much of anything, unless it's tactical of course.' Ron winked. 'Going to suck up to Williams and soften him up?'

'You're wasted as a cabbie.' Jago wished the words unsaid as Ron's jaw tightened and his smile disappeared. 'I didn't mean to insult you. You do a great, worthwhile job. I — '

'You're only saying what the wife

does. She's always telling me to go back to school and finish my degree. Set an example for the kids. Goes on and on about it.'

'And?'

'The darn woman's right. So are you.'

'But you're not taking any notice of us?'

Ron shrugged. 'Maybe more than you think.' He flashed a mischievous grin. 'Bit like you telling me to keep my mouth shut about the pretty lady at Red Roof Farm. Sinks in, doesn't it?'

'Perhaps.'

'For now we'll call it quits. One gourmet breakfast coming up. We can have another go at each other later.' Ron laughed and pulled into the restaurant's drive-through lane.

It'd been necessary to cross the Atlantic to discover people who saw through his outer shell, and Jago wasn't sure if the idea amused, annoyed or pleased him.

★ ★ ★

'Why didn't you mention this adorable man before? I can't believe you hid it from your best friend. I thought we told each other everything,' Lola complained. Two cocktails were all it'd taken for her to spill the beans. 'Pictures. You must have pictures.'

Reluctantly, Meg pulled out her phone and scrolled through to find a few they'd taken in Florence.

'OMG, he's gorgeous. All that dark brooding yumminess, and a cute British accent. Oh be still my beating heart.' Lola sighed. 'If I wasn't a happily married woman, I'd fight you for him. So what's all this nonsense about keeping away from each other? Are you both idiots?' She touched Meg's hand. 'I've never seen you this animated and sparkling when talking about any man.'

'It's not . . . straightforward.'

'Never is.'

'But you and Jack — '

'Do you seriously think it was a piece of cake?'

'Wasn't it?'

Lola picked up her drink and drained it in one large gulp. 'You're crazy. I had to get him out of the clutches of Mary Beth Ringling first.'

Meg couldn't believe she'd forgotten about Jack's assistant, who'd been determined to snag the handsome, wealthy banker and get him down the aisle. There'd been one pivotal weekend when Lola had high-tailed it to Chattanooga and laid down a challenge for her old boyfriend, who'd been inundating her with phone calls and texts without making his intentions clear.

'I told him in not-very-polite terms to either put a ring on my finger or I'd leave him in Mary Beth's not-so-tender grasp.' Lola fixed Meg with a hard stare. 'Don't you dare tell me it's different for you and Jago. Of course it is in some ways, but it's obvious you're seriously attracted to him — so put up a fight.'

'But there's more to it than simply being attracted to each other. That's almost the easy part.'

'It's your turn to buy the drinks — and while you're at it, order a ton of greasy food to soak it up. Then you'll tell me everything about Jago Merryn — and I mean everything.' Lola's eyes flashed. 'When I pack you off home tomorrow, you'll be all set to tackle your Englishman and bring him to heel.'

Meg gave in. With fresh martinis in hand and a platter of cheese sticks, spicy chicken wings and onion rings in front of them, they reverted to their college days. Between eating and drinking, Meg managed to get out the whole story. 'What do you think?'

'I think Mr. Jago Merryn is in a lot of trouble. He doesn't *want* to want you, but he does — badly. Plus he's seeing possibilities in keeping the barbecue business afloat, but doesn't want to do that either. Poor man.' Her wicked smile didn't indicate much in the way of sympathy.

'You haven't changed a bit.' Meg

laughed. 'You might appear to be a respectable wife and mother, but you're the same conniving gal underneath.' She touched her friend's arm. 'You don't know how pleased that makes me.'

'Good. At least I think it is.' Lola grinned. 'Promise me one thing.'

'What?'

'You won't leave it five years before coming to see me again.'

Meg threw her arms around her old friend. 'I won't. And you must come to Franklin. Mom and Dad would love to see y'all.'

'We will.' Lola knocked back the rest of her martini. 'Now get me another drink, and then find a better excuse than I've heard so far to justify not making a move on this gorgeous guy.'

15

'Drop me off here,' Jago ordered the taxi driver.

'You sure? It's a big hike up to the house.'

He'd decided to walk up the long driveway, arrive at his own pace and give himself the chance to check out the lie of the land before officially joining the party. 'Not a problem.'

'What about going back to Nashville?'

Jago frowned. He wasn't sure how things would turn out. 'I'll call if I need a ride.' Thrusting a handful of money at the driver, he walked off with the gravel crunching under his feet. He approached the final corner and caught the drift of laughter and barbecue smoke in the air. As soon as the house came into sight he spotted, and heard, Betty Lou on the porch. His mother stood next to her deep in conversation. The two women hitting it off couldn't be good news.

'There he is. Woo-hoo, Jago, we're here,' Betty Lou yelled and waved at him.

He raised his hand and took a short cut across the grass.

Cecily threw her arms around him and then stepped back to examine him. 'Let me have a good look at you.' The colour left her face.

'What's wrong?'

'Nothing, really.' She shook her head. 'I've simply never seen you looking so much like your father before, that's all.'

Jago guessed she didn't mean it as a compliment.

'You're more tanned and your hair's longer.'

'I suppose.' He refused to continue the difficult conversation with Meg's mother blatantly eavesdropping. 'How was your journey? Where's Ernie?'

Cecily launched into a long-winded story about the horrors of air travel these days and how the inconsiderate customs people confiscated the Cornish pasties she'd brought as gifts for the Harpers. Jago suppressed a smile. The US Customs Service must employ a few brave souls.

'Ernie's over at the barbecue with Gray.' Cecily grinned. 'They're doing the caveman thing with fire and meat. I suspect beer might be involved too.'

'Probably. I'll go and say hello.' No doubt his mother had plenty of questions for him after soaking up all the gossip from Betty Lou, and the longer he could put off answering the happier he'd be. Jago gave his mother a peck on the cheek. 'Won't be long.'

'We'll talk later.' The ominous threat rang in his ears as he made his getaway.

'Might have guessed you'd find your way here.' Gray glanced up from cooking, busy as always with a grill covered with sizzling hamburgers and hot dogs. 'I'm surprised you escaped the women's clutches. They were lying in wait for you.'

'Are there any cold beers going?'

Ernie reached into the cooler and pulled out a can. 'Will this do?'

'Anything will work.'

'Need some Dutch courage?' Gray teased.

'Give me a break,' he light-heartedly protested. 'You're as bad as them.'

Ernie held up his hands in horror. 'Never say that. The Harper men stick together, and you're one by marriage, so we'll let you into the gang.'

'Thanks. I could do with some support.' Jago's fervent reply startled the two men, judging by the instant change in their expressions.

'So Gray was right.'

'In what way?'

His step-father gave him a long, hard stare. 'We're not getting at you.'

'I know. I . . . ' He couldn't lie to either man. 'Sorry.' Jago popped open his beer and took a long swallow. 'I'm guessing you know all about the business I've been working on?'

'Yeah.'

'And?'

Ernie shrugged. 'You wanted to make a change and maybe this is your chance? It could help Meg out too.'

'Perhaps.'

'How about an illegal burger before you face the firing squad again?' Gray slipped a fresh hamburger into a bun. 'We've had ours already.' The cousins broke out laughing and their pale blue eyes glinted with amusement. Their similar stocky build, ruddy faces, and thick brown wavy hair liberally streaked with gray left no doubt as to their relationship.

'Thanks.' Jago added plenty of ketchup and a stack of pickle slices, took a huge bite and chewed, unable to keep from smiling. 'This is one thing you definitely do better here. You'll never find a burger this good in England.'

Gray slapped his shoulder. 'Glad to hear you admit it, son.'

Something tugged on Jago's leg and he glanced down to see Cody Harper grinning up at him.

'We need you to play football. My dad says you won't know how because you only play soccer, but Mom told him you're big and can knock people out of the way.' The boy frowned. 'I can't find Aunt Meg today. She always plays.'

'She does?'

'Yeah. She's fun.'

'I'm afraid Meg is away visiting a friend, but I'll give it a try. Come on.' He took Cody's hand.

'They'll be waiting for you.' Gray nodded towards the porch.

'I'll see them later.' Jago was happy to put it off as long as possible.

* * *

'What's holding you both back? I don't get it.' Lola didn't mince words. 'Are you seriously telling me you came back home from Italy and forgot him?' Her deep throaty laugh made the other people in the bar stare. 'You've gotta

138

be kidding me, Meg. I know you too well.'

'I remembered him, okay?' Her face and neck flamed. 'When he turned up again I was confused. Suddenly there he is as some sort of step-cousin and calling himself by a different name. Are you satisfied now?'

'Maybe. What about him?'

'I'm guessing the same.' She cracked a smile.

'What's his excuse for being skittish?'

Meg took another drink and explained about Jago's parents and his erratic childhood. 'His father left for good when he was a teenager and he hasn't seen him since. I guess it's left him with a jaded view of commitment.' She hated for Lola to think badly of Jago. 'He's a good, kind man, and I'm sure he'd never want to put a child of his own through anything similar.'

'You must've really gotten to him in Florence.'

'Why do you say that?'

Lola smirked. 'Because he didn't trust himself to take you on a second date.'

She'd never looked at it that way before. 'Makes sense. It's sad, though.' Lola munched on another onion ring. 'What're you going to do?'

'About what?'

'Are you going to let him return to London without sorting things out? Love's too precious to let slip through your hands.'

Love? Was her friend totally bonkers? One dishonest date in Italy? It wasn't the perfect recipe for romance from where Meg stood.

'You've had one too many cocktails. I barely know him — and don't forget, he's all set to destroy the barbecue business and put me out of a job. Jago will be on the first plane out of Nashville once the deal's wrapped up.'

'You really think so?' Lola grinned. 'I suspect he's as crazy for you as you are for him, and I predict he'll get his act together and come to his senses. He'll realise he can't live without you and will whisk you off to London with him.'

'You've been reading too many fairytales. Your brain's gone soft.' Meg couldn't hash this out any longer. 'Are you ready to head back home?'

'Home? Early, isn't it?'

'Lola, you're yawning, and I am too.' She'd noticed her friend trying to disguise her tiredness only a few moments ago. They'd both had a long day.

'Fine. If that's the way you want to play it.' Lola's eyes flashed. 'I didn't take you for a coward.'

I wish you hadn't used that particular word. She'd accused Jago of the same thing and he hadn't liked it either. The niggling headache that'd been pulling at her for days sharpened its grip. With a sigh she pushed back her chair, and Lola stood up too. They left in silence.

16

'Jago, come here.'

He winced at his mother's imperious command.

'I'm tired, so don't mess me about.' She pointed to the chair next to her.

'As if I'd dare.' The flippancy earned him a glare, and Jago's heart sunk even lower as Betty Lou emerged from the house to join them.

'First you can tell me why you've moved into a hotel when you had lovely rooms here — and don't spin me a ridiculous tale about it being closer to work either. That's nonsense, and we both know it.' Cecily's firm tone left no wiggle room, and Jago resigned himself to telling an approximation of the truth.

'I'm sure you've heard that Meg invested in and works for the company I'm here to do a deal with. I decided it was wiser for both our sakes for me to move out.' He picked his words carefully, not wanting to put any of the burden on Meg for what'd happened.

'From what Betty Lou said, you've been romancing your cousin.'

'Meg is *not* my cousin.'

'Fine. Have you been romancing Meg-who's-not-your-cousin?'

Jago couldn't help smiling. 'Sort of.'

'You either have or you haven't. Spit it out.'

Betty Lou watched him avidly. He might as well put up his answer in flashing neon lights on a billboard in the centre of Nashville.

'We're two grown people. We flirted a bit. Okay?'

'That's it?'

'Sort of,' Jago muttered. He needed to end this conversation before he accidentally mentioned Italy. 'The rest is no one else's business but ours. Don't get mad at me, but you really need to stay out of this.'

'Betty Lou's been telling us a lot about this business deal you're working on.' Cecily changed tack. 'She says you're tearing apart an old Nashville business that's been around forever for no good reason.'

God preserve him from people who knew a few facts and made up their own story around them. 'It's not that clear-cut. You know I've been involved in this line of work for years and it's never bothered you before.'

'Leave the boy alone, Ceci,' Ernie interrupted, using his pet name for Jago's mother. He trudged up the porch steps, followed close behind by Gray. 'He knows his business better than you do. If he wants our help he'll ask for it. Won't you?' His gaze fixed on Jago.

'I sure will. Thanks.' He hoped his step-father understood the gratitude covered far more than the offer of help on this occasion. Cecily wasn't the only one who'd struck gold when she married Ernie.

'It's time we got to bed. I'm droppin' on my feet.' Ernie yawned. 'We'll see you tomorrow, Jago, if you've got any free time.'

He thought fast. The last thing he needed was to be here when Meg returned. 'I'd love to treat you to lunch in Nashville. You too, of course.' He nodded to Betty Lou and Gray. 'It'll be a small repayment for your hospitality.'

'Sounds good,' Gray agreed for them all. 'How about the Opryland Hotel?' The huge opulent hotel was popular with tourists and locals alike.

'I'll book a table and let you know what time.' Jago quickly stood up.

'I'll run you back to Nashville,' Gray offered.

He swore under his breath. He'd been stupid enough to mention getting a taxi earlier, and now it'd be awkward to refuse the offer of a lift. Betty Lou had been whispering to her husband a couple of minutes ago, which no doubt meant Jago was in for another grilling.

'Thanks, that'd be great.' *Liar*. Gray's quirky smile said he'd read his mind. 'Let's go.'

* ★ ★ ★

Instead of making a fruitless attempt to sleep, Meg turned on her laptop and worked on fresh ideas to bring the failing barbeque sauce into the twenty-first century. Around sunrise she fell into bed, but the adrenaline buzz from her successful brainstorming session wouldn't allow her to unwind. She pulled out her phone and sent Elliott a quick text, then turned out the light and attempted to get comfortable, but through a haze of tiredness she heard her phone beep.

You're brilliant. I should marry you! Meet me at my apartment tonight to discuss? E.

A niggle of doubt flitted through her head, but she told herself he was simply being friendly and making a joke. *Okay. Seven p.m.?*

Fine. See you later. Hugs and kisses. E.

Hugs and kisses? Meg chided herself for nitpicking over Elliott's words. They'd

146

always been affectionate friends. She turned off the phone, rolled over and buried her head under the pile of pillows to block out the daylight streaming into the room.

* * *

'Aunt Meg, wake up. Daddy's cooking pancakes.'

Tiny fingers poked into her back. She opened one eye and glanced over her shoulder at Taylor and Zoe, bright-eyed, full of life and giggling as if she was the funniest thing they'd ever seen.

'Daddy says you have to eat a plain pancake first before you get a chocolate chip one the same as us,' Taylor announced. 'Come on. We're starving.'

'Is your mommy awake?'

'She's been up for ages,' Zoe proclaimed.

Meg felt sorry for her old friend, who must be exhausted after their evening out. *Really. Sorry? Don't lie. You're envious.* Deep down she craved a family of her own, but only when the right man came along. *Maybe he already has* . . . Jago leapt back into her head and she almost screamed with frustration.

She dragged herself up to a sitting position and raked her hands through her hair. 'Give me five minutes and I'll be in the kitchen. Save some for me.' Meg shooed the children out of the room so she could go to the bathroom and brush her teeth in peace. A wonderful tempting aroma of pancakes being cooked drifted in, and she shoved all her other thoughts to one side.

Priorities were important, and right now breakfast was top of the list.

* * *

A summer haze hung over the city, and Jago wished he had a free day to do as he chose. It certainly wouldn't include putting on a suit and tie again and hosting Sunday lunch. Gray's subtle warning hammered in his brain.

Don't get me wrong. You're a fine man. I know Meg's a grown woman, but she's still my little girl. I'm only asking you one thing — don't start something you have no intention of seeing through.

Jago didn't resent Gray for interfering. His own words about flirting with Meg had been repeated back at him, along with the comment about the rest being no one else's business. He'd tried to reassure her father of his intentions, but it'd been hard when he wasn't sure what they were.

You sell yourself short. You're not your father. Learn from his mistakes and carve your own path.

He hadn't contradicted Gray, but deep down wasn't sure he believed him.

Jago skipped the lift and took the stairs instead. A wave of sweltering heat hit him in the face the second he stepped outside to look for his taxi.

'Morning, sir.' Ron stood by the gleaming black car with the door open, grinning at Jago.

'What in heaven's name are you doing here?'

'Charming, I'm sure. It's great to be appreciated.'

'I thought you didn't work week-ends.'

Ron smirked. 'Only for special clients.'

'I am privileged.' Jago's dry response made the other man laugh.

'Get in the car or you'll be late. I'm not breaking the speed limit and getting a ticket for your sake.'

He followed orders because it was easier than arguing.

'Are you having lunch with the family today?'

Jago explained the set-up and found himself telling Ron about yesterday's get-together. When he'd finished he couldn't help smiling. 'You're a good listener. Does it come with the job?'

'Yes and no. Some want to talk, some don't. The knack is working out which camp people fall into.' He shrugged. 'You're different.'

'Don't get sentimental on me or we're doomed,' Jago teased.

Ron pulled the car over onto the exit ramp. 'Five minutes and we'll be there.'

'Have you got any advice on how to handle this lunch?'

'Do some listening yourself. You can learn from people who've been around a while.' He glanced over at Jago. 'Don't be too quick to dismiss their suggestions either.' Ron flashed a wide smile. 'Your agony uncle's done moralising for the day.' He pulled the car through the drop-off outside the main hotel door. 'Have a good lunch and call me when you want to go back.'

'Thanks.'

'No problem. Out you get.' Ron waved him away.

'Yes, sir.' Jago jumped out of the car. Whatever Ron possessed should be bottled and sold. Empathy. Friendship. Honesty. They were straightforward qualities but very rare.

'On the way back we'll talk about how you're gonna win that woman over,' Ron called out.

Jago laughed and shook his head in mock despair. He whistled as he headed for the revolving glass doors.

17

Meg sucked in several deep breaths and forced herself to get out of the car and cross the street to Elliott's apartment building. She pushed open the front door, and the second she stepped inside Elliott jumped up from one of the sofas in the lobby and hurried over to throw his arms around her.

'You're looking pretty today. That blue shirt really suits you.'

'Thanks. Were you waiting for me?' Meg took a step backwards, forcing him to drop his hands away.

'Yes.'

'That was thoughtful,' Meg said automatically.

'Let's go up.' Elliott rested his hand on the hollow of her back as they walked towards the lift. 'All the ideas you sent look great. I can't wait to go over them after dinner.'

'Dinner?'

His bright green eyes gleamed. 'I assumed you'd be hungry. Is that a problem?'

'Of course not.' Something about Elliott's barely suppressed enthusiasm bothered her, although logically he'd done nothing to warrant her suspicion. A flash of annoyance ran through her at all the people who'd tried to spoil her relationship with her old friend.

'I've got in all of your favourites. Lobster mac and cheese from Georgio's with salad and garlic bread. A good bottle of chilled Chardonnay.' He smiled. 'Plus of course chocolate lava cake, courtesy of yours truly, for dessert.' It was his only culinary claim to fame and he'd often joked about learning to make it purely to impress the ladies. Over the years they'd often laughed about their shared lack of prowess in the kitchen.

'You shouldn't have gone to all this trouble. I mustn't stay too late because I've had a busy weekend, and tomorrow morning will roll around quickly.'

The lift stopped and they walked together towards his door. 'I'll stick the macaroni and cheese and bread in the oven to warm up while you make yourself at home.'

'Maybe I could come into the kitchen and help?' Meg offered, following him inside.

'No thanks, I'm good.'

She strolled across the room, stopping to run a finger over the back of the cream leather couch they'd chosen together. When he'd moved in, Elliott had pleaded with her to help him decorate, and the apartment was stamped throughout with her own unique taste.

'Dinner's ready.'

'Wonderful.' Meg's confidence faltered as she approached the mahogany dining table. The long oval table was polished to a gleaming shine and laid with the elegant white china, silver cutlery and sparkling crystal wineglasses they'd bought on their numerous shopping trips. 'Everything looks beautiful.' She dredged up a smile. 'Let's talk about Mama Belle's while we eat and that way we'll be finished quicker.' Meg sat down, pulled out her phone and found the list she'd worked on last night.

'Will you listen to me for a minute first?' Elliott pleaded. 'I'm pretty sure you won't want to hear this, but I'm going to say it anyway.' He sucked in an audible breath. 'I'm tired of pretending to be your 'best friend'. I've loved you since we were little kids.'

She stared at him in shock. 'Don't be — '

'Please don't call me silly,' he begged. Elliott stood by her chair and rested a hand on her shoulder. 'You always berate me for not being more decisive, so for once I'm telling you *exactly* how I feel.' He bent down and kissed the back of her neck.

All Meg could think was that everyone had been right. How could she have been so blind?

The riverfront teemed with people making the most of the cooler evening temperatures. Jago bought a triple-scoop chocolate marshmallow ice cream from one of the food trucks and sprawled on the grass. For the sake of his health and his clothes, it was as well he didn't intend to linger in Nashville, because the ice cream and hamburgers were hard to resist. He idly watched the barges and pleasure boats going up and down the Cumberland River in front of him.

Lunch had gone well, and everyone had enjoyed a good meal before wandering around the hotel and checking out the exotic indoor gardens and fancy shops. Nobody had mentioned Meg, but it hadn't make her any less present. Jago had faced her parents across the table and seen her lingering in her father's smile and her mother's sharp eyes.

He'd used impending work as an

excuse to get out of promising to go back to Red Roof Farm over the next couple of days. Jago knew only too well that Betty Lou and his mother would tug on his string whenever they decided to reel him back in.

His phone buzzed, and for a second he considered ignoring it, but glanced at the screen and saw Gray's number. 'What's up?'

'Nothing much.'

'But?'

'I don't suppose you've heard from Meg?'

Jago sighed. 'No. Look. I thought I made it clear. I — '

'Cool it. I'm not gettin' at you.' Gray hurried on. 'Lola called because Meg left her house around two and promised to let her know when she got back to Franklin, and she's heard nothing.'

'Isn't she answering her phone?'

'Nope. It's going straight to voice-mail.' An edge of worry tinged Gray's voice. 'Don't suggest calling the police. They'll only say she's a grown woman and we've got no reason to believe she's in any danger.'

'That's the truth, Gray. I expect her phone battery is dead. She probably stopped somewhere to go shopping.' He tried to laugh. 'It's what women do.'

'I'm sure you're right.'

'If she gets in touch I'll be sure to let you know. I'm heading back to my hotel soon, and I'll be in all the rest of the evening doing some work. Call anytime.' Gray thanked him and rang off.

While he'd been talking, the ice cream had melted down over his hand, and Jago tossed the remains in the nearest rubbish bin. Meg wasn't the type to let the people she loved worry about her unnecessarily. The lame shopping excuse was the best he could come up with, but deep down Jago knew she would've rung if she planned to be late.

He racked his brain as he hurried back to his hotel and tried to remember everything Gray told him about Meg's friend Lola. Jago had connected her name in his head with the famous Barry Manilow song about whatever Lola wants, Lola gets. Lola's surname escaped him, but he'd start by doing a search of University of Tennessee alumni for the year Meg graduated. He hurried into the lobby and ran upstairs to his room.

It didn't take long. Lola Carothers née Maddison. Married to Jack and now living in Chattanooga. *Bingo*. Jago tapped in her phone number and mentioned his name as soon as she answered in case she thought he was a nuisance caller and hung up.

'Wow, you're keener than I thought.'

'Excuse me?'

'Meg's told me *all* about you.'

'Really?' *Stupid*. Of course she'd talk to her best friend about what was bothering her. Namely him.

'What can I do for you?' Her light southern drawl, laced with good humour, trickled down the line.

Jago stuck to the basics and explained Gray's concern over his daughter. 'She

160

didn't mention stopping anywhere on the way back, did she?' He appreciated the fact Lola didn't answer straight away but gave it some thought.

'No. But I could tell there were things on her mind. Apart from you, that is.'

He struggled not to seem impatient.

'I'm not sure how much I should say.'

'I'm simply concerned about Meg's welfare, and so is her family. I'm not going to freak out if you tell me she's visiting another man.' *I'd hate it but I'd suck it up.*

'Don't be blind. There's only you, but you're both too dumb to see it.'

Jago's voice deserted him.

'Oops, sorry, I shouldn't have said that.' Lola's giggle swiftly faded away. 'She kept saying she's letting Elliott down by not coming up with ideas to save the barbecue sauce company.'

'Do you think she might've gone to see him?' Jago's mind raced.

'I guess she might've. She still refuses to admit that he's got a crush on her, but the man's loved her forever. Everybody else sees it except her. Meg seemed calmer this morning, as though she'd come to a decision.' Lola hesitated. 'I hoped it was to do with you, but obviously that isn't the case.'

'Thanks. You've been a huge help. I'll call her parents and let you know when we find anything out.'

'She said you were a good man.'

Jago swallowed hard.

'I hope she's right. Keep in touch. Bye.'

He immediately entered Gray's number. 'I have something. At least I might. Listen to this.' He told Meg's father about his conversation with Lola.

'Would you mind going over to Elliott's apartment and making sure she's there?' Gray pleaded.

'Are you sure? Meg might get mad.'

'I'll take the blame.'

A lot of good that'll do when she scalps me. 'All right. I'll go.' Jago asked for Elliott's address. 'If you don't hear from me within an hour, send in the cops,' he joked. 'It'll mean she's killed me for sticking my nose in where I'm not wanted.'

'As long as she's okay, does it matter?' Gray asked, and Jago had to agree. He'd never forgive himself otherwise.

18

'Marry me, Meg. We were meant to be together.'

'Marry you? But you're my best friend,' Meg blurted out, unable to hide her shock.

'Don't they say all the best marriages start with friendship?'

'Yes, but there's got to be something — '

'More?' Elliott asked. 'There's a heck of a lot more already on my side. Always has been. I'm not rushing you. I don't need an answer tonight. How about we enjoy our meal and talk about work afterwards?'

'I ought to call my folks. They'll wonder where I am.'

'Would you mind waiting until after dinner?'

'I suppose not.'

'Eat up.' Elliott left her to sit back down.

'I'm sorry you've gone to all this trouble, but I ate a big lunch and I'm not really hungry.' She couldn't tell him the truth — that his out-of-the-blue proposal had killed her appetite.

'You'll eat dessert.'

'Maybe.'

His familiar smile returned. 'You never turn down my chocolate lava cake.'

A loud knock rapped on the door.

'Ignore it,' he insisted. 'I don't want to spoil our time together.'

'What if it's someone important?'

'Fine. I'll go and check.' Elliott's reluctance was obvious. 'I'll be right back.'

The sooner she could manage to get away the better.

'Merryn!' Elliott exclaimed when he opened the door. 'What are you doing here?'

Jago managed a friendly smile in the face of Elliott's obvious surprise. 'I've put together a few business proposals and wanted to discuss them privately before tomorrow morning. Is it all right if I come in?' He brushed past without waiting for a response and spotted Meg sitting at a fully laid dining table, her face pale and strained. 'I didn't realise you had company. Hello, Miss Harper.' Jago hoped she'd play along. 'I'm sorry for the interruption.'

'It's not a problem,' Elliott said. 'Meg came over for dinner and we were about to go over a few ideas she's got to help the business — weren't we, sweetheart?'

Sweetheart? 'Yes, we were. Please join us.' The plea in her voice tugged at Jago.

'Would you like a drink?' Elliott picked up the wine bottle.

'I'd prefer a beer if you've got one.'

'Meg, would you do the honours?'

'Of course.' She stood up and threw Jago a worried glance behind Elliott's back.

'What's with all the 'Mr. Merryn' thing anyway? I thought we agreed you were going to call me Jago outside of work?'

'I've changed my mind. I'd prefer to keep things between us on a business footing. After all, we're not really friends, are we?' Elliott's harsh tone contrasted with his normal easy drawl.

Meg returned and passed over a cold can of beer to Jago. 'Why don't we all have dessert and share our ideas?' she suggested. 'Elliott makes the most wonderful chocolate lava cake.'

'That sounds delicious.'

'I suppose we could.' Elliott conceded. 'I'll get it ready. And please don't offer to help, Meg dear — remember, you ruined it last time. It's supposed to be soft and runny inside, not hard as a rock.' He glanced at Jago with a conspiratorial smile. 'This lovely lady and cooking don't go together well. I'm no star in the kitchen, but she's worse.'

Jago knew it wasn't the right moment to mention the delicious barbecued ribs.

'I won't be long. The cakes only take a few minutes in the microwave. Why don't you make yourselves comfortable on the sofa and we'll eat over there.'

'I'll show Mr. Merryn the view first. Everyone needs to see Nashville from this high up.' Meg slipped her hand through Jago's arm and led him away.

The huge unadorned window looked out over the dramatic skyline of the city, but Jago focused on making the most of their few minutes alone. He kept his voice low and told Meg about his phone calls with her father and Lola.

'I only came here to talk business,' Meg whispered, 'but Elliott turned strange on me. He started to say all this crazy stuff about always having loved me and wanting to marry me.'

Jago's mind raced. 'Go along with whatever I say in a minute. I think I've got a solution.'

'I'm very glad you're here.'

Me too.

'All right, you two, dessert is ready.' Elliott came back out of the kitchen carrying a loaded tray and set it down on the glass coffee table. 'So what are these famous proposals, Mr. Merryn?'

'Am I right in thinking that you and the other partners who are interested in saving the company are short of available cash?'

'Yes. What about it?'

'I'm prepared to consider helping you out if the terms are right.'

Elliott frowned. 'We can't get entangled in a high-interest loan. We're all in enough debt already.'

'That's not what I'm getting at. I'm offering to buy shares in the restructured business. My money and expertise, combined with your local knowledge, could be a win-win situation for us all.'

'But why would you be interested? This isn't your usual method of operation.'

Jago started to talk about the changes he was hoping to make in his working life and couldn't help noticing how intently Meg was listening to him. 'The only thing is that I need you to contact your friends tonight and float my idea to them. I must have an answer before nine o'clock tomorrow morning.'

He kept his fingers crossed that Elliott's passion for his family's barbecue business would trump trying to win over Meg.

19

'Why don't we go away and leave you to it so you can make your phone calls?' Meg hurried to suggest. 'I think my input will be of more use once the decision's been made one way or the other.'

'It certainly would,' Jago agreed. 'Would you mind giving me a lift back into town? I let my taxi go.'

'Of course. It'd be happy to. I'm parked right outside.' Meg walked back to the table and collected her phone and handbag.

'But Meg,' Elliott started to protest, 'we've got a lot to — '

'There's plenty of time. I'll see you at work.'

Jago took a gentle hold of Meg's arm. 'I'll look forward to hearing from you, and I really hope we can work things out.' He steered her towards the door and on outside while Elliott shouted goodbye after them. 'Are you okay?'

'I think so.' Meg shrugged. 'A bit stunned, that's all.'

'Good. Let's get out of here.' Over by the lift, Jago wrapped his arm around her shoulder and she didn't push him away. 'You'd better give your family a ring.'

'I will, but I'm really not ready to go back to Red Roof yet.'

'How about we get some coffee at the Renaissance Hotel? It's not too far from here.'

Meg nodded. 'That sounds good.'

As they stepped outside, Jago let go of Meg. 'We don't want to antagonise Elliott if he's watching.'

'Smart man.'

'I try.'

She unlocked the car. 'What a day.' She appreciated the fact that Jago didn't talk on the short drive, and they were soon at the hotel.

She couldn't help staring at him across the table. There'd been no fresh haircut since he'd arrived, and his thick black hair fell down well over his collar, giving him a rakish look. Combined with the darker tan he'd acquired in the Nashville heat, it deepened the effect of his Mediterranean good looks.

'I know you promised me coffee, but I could do with something stronger,' Meg declared. 'I'll have a Jack Daniels on the rocks please.'

Jago raised one eyebrow but didn't argue. 'Certainly.' He headed over to the bar, and she shamelessly watched the play of his muscles under his dark green T-shirt and the way his jeans fitted perfectly. *Hey, you admire his sharp intelligence and his good sense of humour too. You're human. Give yourself a break.*

'There you go.' He set a glass in front of her and sat back down on the soft black leather sofa, casually resting one long leg up on the other knee. 'Do you want to talk about Elliott?'

Meg took a sip of her whisky.

'Actually if you don't mind, before

you start I need to tell you something.' He cleared his throat and a flush of colour sharpened his cheekbones. 'I've moved out of Red Roof and I'm staying here at the Renaissance now.'

'Why?'

Jago played with a used napkin on the table, ripping it into shreds as he spoke. 'The business link between us makes it awkward and . . . our parents have picked up on the attraction between us. I got a friendly word of warning from your father.'

'Oh, for heaven's sake. Anyone would think we were teenagers.'

'It's okay. I get where he's coming from.' He held out his hand. 'Would you mind sitting over here with me?'

Wordlessly she got up and perched on the seat next to him, only relaxing when he slid his arm around her shoulder and eased her back to rest against his chest.

'I must've been sending out the wrong signals to Elliott,' she blurted out.

'You mustn't blame yourself.'

'How would you feel if a woman basically fainted in shock when you proposed to her?'

Jago's features darkened. 'I would never propose to any woman unless I believed she loved me back heart and soul.' His vehemence took her aback. 'He knew you didn't feel that way about him but he still went ahead.'

Meg couldn't argue.

'Your ought to tell your parents just so it's out in the open.' He kissed her cheek, and the waft of his familiar cologne brought back memories of their first embrace under the shadow of the Duomo in Florence. 'You weren't tempted to accept? Elliott is a good-looking, intelligent man who'd make a decent husband.'

'Of course not!'

'I suppose you want the fairytale.'

'Is that so terrible?'

Jago gave a slight shrug. 'I suppose not if you believe in them.'

'You don't?' she probed, wanting to

dig deeper and find out who Jago Merryn really was deep inside.

'When the palace reverberates with the sound of Cinderella and Prince Charming arguing day after day and the prince eventually rides off on his white horse and doesn't return, it tends to make you cynical. I'd rather believe in a goose laying golden eggs.'

His jaundiced view of love took her breath away. Jago wouldn't want her heart if she offered it to him, and that sad knowledge chilled her to the core.

'Thanks for the advice.' She abandoned her drink and jumped up. 'I'll see you in the morning.'

'Meg, I'm — '

'Don't worry. It's not a problem.' She cut him off before her resolve weakened. 'Thanks again for your help tonight.' She hurried out of the lounge and refused to look back. She'd done far too much of that already.

Jago forced himself to stay seated and not run after Meg. In Florence she'd given him a glimpse of a possibility he'd never imagined for himself, but after only one date he'd known that a casual relationship would never be enough with Meg and that had scared him. When he'd come face to face with her again a few weeks ago, he'd experienced a brief foolish hope that he'd been given another chance, but he'd come to his senses. *Matter of opinion.*

When she was out of sight, he headed up to his room. He ordered room service and settled down with his laptop to run through the figures for tomorrow's meeting.

Properties for sale in Franklin. Why did he type that in? He entered the address of the house he'd spotted on his bicycle ride into Franklin and waited. Magnolia Glade was the nearest neighbour to Red Roof Farm and sat on fifty-seven acres of prime farmland. Jago started to watch a short online tour around the house, and he couldn't help wondering what it would be like to live there. *Are you out of your mind?* But there was no logical reason why he shouldn't live wherever he chose. He loved Cornwall deeply, but hadn't lived there since he'd left at eighteen. His mother was comfortably settled now, leaving him free to do as he wished.

Jago fired off an email to the agent and requested a tour of the property.

'Room service, Mr. Merryn.'

'Come in.' He tipped the waiter before absentmindedly wolfing down a juicy hamburger while he read the agent's prompt response. He supposed that anyone showing interest in a $3.5 million property on a Sunday evening got that sort of attention. He decided to finish his dinner before calling the agent back, because it never did in his business to show too much enthusiasm.

Does the same trick work on women?

He hadn't hidden his interest in Meg when they'd first met, but where had that got him? *In love?* Jago squirted ketchup over the pile of golden crispy fries and crammed a handful into his mouth. After a few minutes he pushed the empty plate to one side and picked up the phone. Soon he'd arranged to be at Magnolia Glade after he finished work the next day. He decided to celebrate by retrieving a bottle of beer from the mini-bar, but the phone rang before he could take a drink.

'Good evening, Elliott. Have you got some news for me?'

'I sure do, but I also found out a few things about you and Meg tonight.'

'In what way?'

'You're the reason she turned me down, aren't you? I saw the way the two of you looked at each other earlier.'

Jago didn't want to mess up the business deal at this late stage and chose his next words very carefully.

20

Exhaustion swamped Meg to the point where she couldn't answer any more of her parents' questions. 'Look, I'm fine. Please leave it.'

'Thanks to Jago. We owe that boy,' her father persisted.

Meg managed not to roll her eyes. 'This is Elliott we're talking about, not Godzilla. Be realistic, Dad. Goodnight.'

'Jago's a good, solid man,' her mother declared, making him sound like a desirable piece of furniture.

'For goodness sake, give it a break, Mom.'

'I'm just saying. Think about it. He's obviously crazy about you.'

Meg walked away before she could be tempted to answer back.

'Your dad agrees with me,' Betty Lou called out after her.

I'll bet he does. He's had enough

practice. She hurried upstairs to her bedroom and slammed the door behind her. She didn't bother to unpack, and took a quick shower before jumping straight into bed. Before she could close her eyes, her phone beeped.

Call me ASAP. Elliott knows. JM.

Meg called him back right away. 'What's up?'

'I'm really sorry. This is all my fault.'

'What is?'

Jago sighed. 'I went golfing with Clayborne Williams yesterday and I ran out of things to talk about. I said about staying at Red Roof Farm and threw in the fact that my mother and your family were related. When Elliott rang around everyone tonight to talk about a possible deal, he mentioned having dinner with you, and my old friend Clayborne dropped that little snippet of news about us into the conversation.'

Meg sighed. 'Don't worry. I'll give Elliott a call and tell him the truth — minus any mention of Florence, which is none of his business. I'll say the fact we're sort-of-related is no big deal and act surprised that he didn't already know.'

'I'm afraid that's not going to work,' Jago murmured. 'Elliott guessed there's . . . something between us, and accused me of wrecking his chances with you. I told him the truth about us having met before.'

'Did you have to?'

'Oh Meg, what does it matter in the long run? You don't want to marry the man. So what if we went on one date? It's not a big deal.'

The fact that he was right didn't make his casual dismissal of their relationship any more palatable. Jago must never realise how much he meant to her. 'How did he react?'

'Three guesses.'

'I'm sure Elliott said what a great guy you are, insisted you'd be perfect for me, and wished us every happiness.'

'Of course.' Jago's rich warm laughter trickled down the phone.

'But what about the deal? Did he

manage to pull something off?'

'He certainly did. Luckily his desire to keep Mama Belle's afloat inched out his resentment, and he convinced enough of the board members to accept my offer.' His voice hitched. 'But it comes with one condition.'

'Let me take a wild guess. I'm to have nothing to do with it.'

'He wants to buy out your share. He's hurt, Meg, and you're the obvious target.'

'I know.' She felt awful. 'Well you can easily find someone else to do the PR side, and I'll give you some recommendations if you want. As long as I get my money back, I'm good. That's the least of my worries right now.'

'Is it vain of me to think I'm the cause of most of them?' Sorrow ran through his deep voice and a lump formed in her throat. 'Don't answer me now, Meg. Go to bed. You must be tired and it's late.'

She said good night and hung up, only wishing she could have been honest with him for once. She threw herself on the bed, and the tears she'd held back all day finally flowed.

* * *

Jago stood at his hotel room window and watched the sun rise over Nashville. Last night the conversations he'd had with Elliott and Meg ran circles around his head. He hadn't been able to express to Meg how sorry he'd felt for Elliott when the man's love for her shone through his bitterness.

'You haven't got a clue, Merryn,' he'd said. 'You don't know the meaning of the word 'love'. You're a selfish man who takes what he wants and moves on with no thought to those you leave behind. I don't know how long your interest in our company will last, but I'd take a bet on the fact you'll be gone in six months. But if you help save Mama Belle's, I'll take your money and shout for joy when you leave.'

Jago hadn't argued with Elliott

because he was right on so many levels. Luckily no one realised the anguish it had caused Jago to stand Meg up in Italy on their second date. She'd filled his head for months afterwards, and he couldn't count the number of times he'd picked up the phone to ring her or the emails he'd written before hitting the 'delete' button.

That morning he'd put on his usual smart suit and his best business game-face before juggling a few numbers and getting another deal signed. He'd never pulled a company back from the brink before, and the follow-up could be a huge challenge.

He pulled on his running clothes. Maybe if he pounded out a few miles and worked off some of his excess energy, he would settle down. He grabbed his phone, room key card and a bottle of cold water before making his way downstairs.

'Ah, Mr. Merryn,' the receptionist called across to him as he stepped out of the lift. 'There's a . . . gentleman looking for you.'

Jago glanced around the deserted lobby. 'Does this gentleman have a name?'

'If he does, he wouldn't give it to me.' The man's arch reply made him smile. 'He was here about an hour ago, but I declined to call you that early unless it was an emergency. He said he'd return this evening.'

'Could you describe him to me?'

'Short stocky build, dark gray hair, outdoor-tanned skin.'

The description didn't ring a bell with Jago. 'I won't be back until at least seven tonight. If this person returns, could you ask whoever is on the desk to get a name or phone number?'

'We'll do our best, sir.'

Jago thanked him and headed outside.

'Lucca?'

He jerked around at the sound of his name and his legs threatened to crumple underneath him. '*Babbo?*'

186

21

The childish name for his father automatically slipped out along with a million memories. Jago scanned over the man standing awkwardly in front of him clutching a worn baseball cap in his hands. He couldn't reconcile the ageing, scruffy man with the handsome, dapper father of his childhood.

'Bit of a surprise, eh?'

Jago found his voice again. 'You could say that. How did you track me down?'

A hint of his father's old charming smile returned. 'It's not hard when you ask the right questions. You live a very public life.'

'Have you been in touch with my mother?' Jago hoped Marco wasn't aware that his ex-wife was in Nashville.

'No.' Marco cracked a wry smile. 'I don't have a death wish. She made it very clear I wasn't to contact either one of you again.'

'When did she say that?'

'The day she sent me away for the last time.'

'Sent you? Don't lie. You left again. The only difference between that and all the other times was the fact that you never came back.'

'Is that what she told you?' Marco shook his head. 'It's no more than I deserve. Don't blame her. I was a lousy husband and father.'

Sweat trickled down Jago's face and he became aware they were attracting attention from the few early-morning walkers and joggers enjoying the empty downtown streets. 'Why don't we take this inside?'

'Are you sure? The hotel might not be keen. I've been living rough while I'm here working and I haven't had a chance to clean up.'

Jago managed a tense smile. 'Trust me, I'm paying them enough. They won't complain. We'll order breakfast to be sent up to my room. Come on.' They walked inside and approached the reception desk. 'Could you have breakfast for two sent to my room please? A selection of food will be fine along with tea and coffee.'

'Life's different when you have money, isn't it?' Marco commented as they headed for the lifts.

'I've worked hard for everything I have,' Jago snapped. 'Something you wouldn't understand.' They didn't speak another word until the lift stopped. 'I won't listen to you saying anything bad about my mother.'

The pain in his father's dark eyes deepened. 'I would never do that. She's a wonderful woman and her new husband is a lucky man.'

Jago couldn't hide his surprise. 'You're right on both counts. Why are you here, anyway?'

'Where to begin is the question.' His father's light tone didn't fool him. 'I don't know about you, but I'm starving. Why don't we wait to talk properly until after we've had some breakfast?'

'Fine.' Jago led the way in. 'You go ahead and sit down while I get changed ready for work.' He retreated to the bedroom and took a quick cool shower. His shaky hands smoothed down his untidy hair and he took several slow, deep breaths before going back out to join his father. 'Help yourself.' He gestured to the trays of food that'd already arrived. Jago picked up a glass of orange juice, but the idea of trying to eat anything tied his stomach in knots.

'This isn't easy for me either, you know,' Marco muttered.

'I don't suppose it is, but you'll have to excuse me if I don't feel too sorry for you.' Twenty years of suppressed anger bubbled out. 'You wrecked my childhood, and at sixteen I was supposed to turn into the man of the house when you left. Did you ever wonder how that affected me?' Jago blinked back tears.

'I'm sorry.'

'Sorry.' Jago's voice rose. 'You seriously think that makes it all right?' He couldn't do this. 'Get out. Now. And don't come back.'

'I don't blame you for — '

'That's generous of you.'

His father flinched at Jago's sarcasm-laced words. 'If you change your mind and want to contact me, here are my details.' Marco pulled out a leather wallet and took out a business card, but when Jago made no move to take it from his outstretched hand he laid it down on the table. He headed towards the door and stopped with his hand on the knob. 'Don't ever forget that I love you. I've thought about you every single day.'

'Please just go.' He sighed, and his weary response finally had an effect. Jago was left alone. Again.

* * *

Meg kept her head down and worked solidly all morning while the directors-only meeting was going on. Lola's constant stream of texts wasn't helping her itchy mood. According to her, the few minutes of conversation she'd shared with Jago made it perfectly clear he adored Meg and would do anything for her. Lola was the consummate dreamer.

She slammed her computer shut, ready to sneak out for some lunch. With the temperature soaring far above normal for July and humidity at record levels, a sensible woman would choose somewhere cool with decent air conditioning; but why spoil her recent track record? She'd walk to her favourite spot in Riverfront Park and gorge on a loaded hot dog and a large glass of fresh, tart lemonade.

She crept down the back stairs and headed outside. She set off at a brisk pace and bought lunch from one of the food carts in the park before settling down on the grass by her favourite shade tree.

'Not hanging out with your boyfriend today?'

'Excuse me?' She glanced up to see

Elliott standing over her.

'You kept your links to Mr. Jago Merryn well hidden.'

'Our family connection was nobody's business, and I'm sure you've been on plenty of dates without feeling the need to tell me about it.'

'Are you?'

Meg ignored his ambiguous question. 'I used my mom's maiden name when I met Jago because I'd heard a lot of stories about being cautious when travelling, and it sunk in. He had no reason to connect me with Red Roof Farm when he was coming to work in Nashville. As far as he was concerned, a relative of his step-father's offered him a bed, and that was the end of the story.'

'You've worked out your tales well, I'll give you that.'

She collected the abandoned remnants of her lunch and stood up. 'I don't have to listen to this. I did nothing wrong and neither did Jago. He's saving your business. You should be grateful to him.'

'Maybe I hate having to be *grateful*.'

'That's your problem. Not mine or Jago's.'

'Yeah, I know.' He shuffled from one foot to the other.

'Did you get the deal signed this morning?'

'Everything is hammered out apart from a few last details that we'll finish up this afternoon.' Elliott glowered. 'It means the majority shareholding will be out of family hands for the first time in a century.'

'At least Mama Belle's won't go into bankruptcy.'

'True.' His eyes glazed over. 'I didn't mean to freak you out yesterday.' He shoved his hands in his pockets.

'I know,' she half-whispered, 'but you did.'

'Yeah. I knew it was a mistake while I was speaking but couldn't stop myself.' He shrugged. 'I needed you to know how much you meant to me.' Elliott's voice broke. 'I don't think I can be simply your friend anymore, Meg. I wish I could. Can you understand?'

'Yes, and I'm truly sorry.'

'I'll always wish the best for you, Meg. I'd hoped it could've been a life with me, but . . . ' His voice trailed away and he stared down at his feet.

'I wish you everything good too, Elliott.'

He dredged up a faint smile before he turned and walked away. For a second Meg almost went after him, but she forced herself to stay where she was. She wrapped up her half-eaten hot dog and got up to toss it into the bin.

She'd better return to her office because she hadn't been fired yet.

22

Magnolia Glade belonged on the front cover of a magazine promoting the virtues of southern living. The late afternoon sun swathed the lush fields with a soft yellow glow, and the house fitted into a slight curve in the land as though it'd been there forever.

Jago struggled to hide his interest from the agent standing next to him but was finally forced to give in. 'It's quite something.'

'It certainly is, sir. The property's been in the Jordan family for over two hundred years. They're descendants of Francis Jordan, who is claimed to be the first settler in Williamson County.' He gave a self-deprecating smile. 'Around here that's ancient history.'

The moment he stopped his rental car by the freshly painted white wood gates, the hassles of the day retreated, and Jago wished Warren Green could go away and leave him to look around by himself. Magnolia Glade could be exactly what he needed for his new life. Of course, it would be even better if he could share it with Meg. *Don't go there*, he told himself.

'The new owner is a distant cousin of the Jordan family who is a native New Yorker. He has no interest in moving and wants it sold as soon as possible.' The man's voice was filled with disdain for someone who could casually abandon their heritage. 'It's a big house for a single man, but perhaps you have plans to change that soon?'

The question struck Jago hard. 'Not at the moment, but maybe in the future.'

'I didn't mean to be intrusive.'

'No problem. I simply want . . . space.'

'Fifty-seven acres will give you plenty of that, sir.'

'It certainly will.' Jago cracked a smile. 'May we go and see the house?'

'Of course.'

They drove in convoy down the long gravel driveway, and vivid memories of arriving at Red Roof Farm grabbed Jago by the throat. Was he trying to recreate something he could never have? The estate agent stopped his car outside the front door and Jago followed suit. They both got out, and Jago stared at the house. He allowed the man's continuing sales spiel to wash over him while he took the time to appreciate the building's quiet beauty. The original house had been extended many times, but always sympathetically, and the combination of weathered red bricks and dark wood suited his simple tastes.

'You may think this is a sales pitch, but I see a lot of properties and they don't make me envious, while this one does.' The man's blunt comment drew a broad smile out of Jago. 'If I had the money I'd buy it myself.'

'Don't worry — I hear a lot of flannel in my line of work, and I know you're not spinning me a tale.'

'Good. Come on, I'll show you around.'

Jago's interest grew over the next hour as they examined every inch of the house. There was a lot of work to be done, because it hadn't been decorated or modernised in decades, but structurally everything was sound. He'd bought plenty of other properties, but this was the first he'd been able to imagine actually living in.

'The farm manager lives in that cottage.' The agent pointed towards a neat red-brick building to the left of the main house. 'He's been paid through the end of the month, but after that he'll have to move out unless a new owner is in place and keeps him on.'

'If I do decide to buy, I'd need someone to run that side of things for me, so if he's any good I'm happy to consider employing him.'

'Fair enough.' Warren Green gestured towards his car. 'How about we take a drive around the rest of the property?'

'Sure.'

By the time they returned to the house, Jago couldn't have said no to Magnolia Glade if he'd tried. 'Put in an offer for me.' He named a figure and the agent's eyebrows rose.

'I was going to suggest ten percent lower, not higher, sir.'

'I don't want to lose it.'

'Magnolia Glade's been on the market for six months and we've brought the price down twice. There haven't been any other offers and the owner is keen to sell.'

'Fine. I'm content to offer more because I want this rushed through. I'm keen to take possession as fast as possible.'

'I'm sure the owner would be agreeable to you renting Magnolia Glade until the paperwork is complete. It's been vacant since the owner passed away at Christmas, and it's never good for a house to stand empty.'

Jago couldn't remember being this excited since he'd completed his first acquisition and bought a small engineering company outside of London before selling it on for triple the price. 'You get this sorted out for me and I'll make it worth your while.'

'I'll have you in by the weekend,' the agent promised.

They parted company and Jago made his way back down to the main road. He'd love to drive over to Red Roof Farm and share his news with the Harper family, but wasn't ready for the complicated explanations it would involve. Going back to Nashville was a much safer bet.

★   ★   ★

'Have you seen Jago today or heard anything from him?' Betty Lou asked.

Meg stopped in the middle of chopping up a cucumber for tonight's salad. 'No. There were board meetings most of the day and they were still at it when I left.'

'Cecily's worried because he hasn't

been in touch since yesterday lunch-time.'

'I'm sure he's been very busy, Mom. Do you know how long Cecily and Ernie are planning to stay?'

'I'm not sure. Ernie was saying they'd probably take off in their rental car tomorrow morning to show Cecily around more of Tennessee. They'll come back here again at the weekend before returning to Cornwall early next week.'

Meg scooped the diced cucumber into a glass bowl before starting on the tomatoes. Grown in their own garden, they were a rich deep red, and their fragrant smell encapsulated summer in her mind.

'You could call Jago and ask if he wants to join us for dinner,' Betty Lou suggested.

'Why don't you call him yourself? Or you could leave the poor man alone and plan something for the weekend instead.'

'You are stubborn sometimes.'

'I wonder who I get that from.'

'I have no idea. It must be your father.'

'Who's takin' my name in vain?' Gray asked, wandering in to join them. Meg had had a quiet word with him earlier and she'd given him brief details of her lunchtime meeting with Elliott. 'How's my favourite daughter?' He planted a kiss on her forehead, and his sympathetic gaze rested on her.

'Considering I'm your only one, that's not saying much,' Meg teased.

Her mother launched into a string of complaints about her unappreciative daughter. 'I was only trying to be friendly and a good hostess.'

'No, you weren't. You're still trying to match-make. Leave them alone,' Gray stated in his normal plain, no-nonsense fashion.

'Fine,' Betty Lou grunted. 'I'm going to pick some herbs. I know when I'm not wanted,' she said with a snort, and bustled out of the back door.

'She means well.'

'Remember you're supposed to say 'bless her heart' afterwards,' Meg added in the backhanded compliment so popular in the south.

Gray grinned and wagged his finger at her in fake disappointment. He picked up a tomato wedge and popped it into his mouth. 'Damn, they're good.' He ate another. 'Sorry. You'll have to cut more.'

'Eat as many as you want.' She glanced down at the cutting board. 'What I'm going to say next needs to stay between you and me. I — '

'Stop right there.' Her father touched her arm. 'I'm lousy at keeping secrets from your mama.'

'Fine. You can tell her later if you have to, but I'm not discussing this in front of Cecily and Ernie.' Before she lost her nerve, Meg told him about meeting Jago in Italy. 'That's it. One date and then he dumped me. We were stupid to keep it a secret.'

'Yeah, you were. 'Honesty is the best policy' might be one of the oldest adages, but that doesn't make it any less valid.' He studied her. 'You love him, don't you? Gray chuckled. 'Heck, he loves you too, doesn't he? You're both dumb.'

'I'm sure he doesn't, Daddy, and thanks for the huge vote of confidence.'

'No problem. What're you gonna do about it?'

'I haven't got a clue,' Meg admitted. 'Any advice?'

'You'll have to tell him how you feel, because men are lousy at mind-reading. If he throws it back in your face, at least you'll know.' He flashed a self-satisfied smile. 'Somehow I don't think he will.'

Her mother breezed back in. 'What are you two up to now?'

'There's something our daughter and Mr. Jago Merryn forgot to mention.'

Meg held her breath as her father started to speak, and waited for Betty Lou's rant to begin.

23

'I owe your Aunt Sarah an apology,' Betty Lou said, glaring at Meg. 'The day Jago arrived, she swore you already knew each other. I told her she'd been sitting out in the sun too long and it'd addled her brain.'

Meg flinched.

'Do Cecily and Ernie know?'

'No. We had our reasons for keeping quiet.'

'Stupid ones,' Betty Lou retorted.

'Gee, don't hold back will you, Mom?'

'You don't deserve it.' She switched her attention back to Gray. 'What are we gonna do about this mess?'

'Do? Nothing.'

'You're not going to help your daughter?'

'Not unless she asks for it.' Gray's steady determination silenced her mother.

'Right now we're gonna finish getting supper ready, and we aren't discussing this around the table either.'

'But they love each other.' Meg smiled at her mother's forthright statement.

'They've got to work it out, not us.' Gray insisted.

'Something smells good,' Ernie said as he wandered into the kitchen, and Meg could've kissed him for his opportune timing. He checked out the pans simmering on top of the cooker. 'Green beans and creamed corn. Let me guess — they're to go with a chicken pot pie?' He nodded to Meg. 'I mentioned to your sweet mother last night that it was a favourite of mine.'

Cecily came in to join them. 'I might've guessed you were hunting up food again. All he's done since we got here is eat. His father used to cook a lot of the old southern favourites, but since he passed Ernie's gone into withdrawal.'

'Unless you need me, I'll leave you to

finish up. I'll be on the porch when it's ready,' Gray ventured.

'Oh, get out from under my feet.' Betty Lou laughed and shooed him away.

'I forgot to tell you something,' Gray said when he reached the door.

'Something else?'

He ignored the dig. 'When I drove past Magnolia Glade I saw a 'sale pending' sticker plastered all over the sign.'

'I can't believe the Jordan boy's lettin' it go. Francis Jordan would turn in his grave,' Betty Lou complained. 'I hope the new owner won't be some highfalutin' music mogul who wants to play at farming and has wild, noisy parties.'

Gray sighed. 'Give them a chance. I hate seeing the old place empty.'

'I'll keep a lookout so we can go over and welcome them soon when they move in.'

'You do that.'

Gray made his escape, and Meg

wished she could do the same.

'Cecily, you can fix everyone's drinks, and I'll take the pie out to cool down for a few minutes,' Betty Lou rattled on while Meg concentrated on transferring the salad to a pretty glass bowl. 'Have you heard from that renegade son of yours?'

'He isn't answering my messages,' Cecily sighed. 'Ernie tells me to leave him alone. I know he's busy, but even so.'

'They always are busy.'

Meg refused to react.

'He's a good son, really. Jago did everything he could to help when his father left, and I don't know what I'd have done without him before I met Ernie. I wish he'd find some nice girl and settle down, but he works too hard, and with all his travelling he's never in one place long enough to romance anyone.'

Meg's cheeks heated and she didn't dare to look up.

'Maybe he'll surprise you one day.'

Keep quiet or Daddy will kill you, Meg thought.

'Any woman would be lucky to have him — wouldn't they, Meg?' said Betty Lou.

'I'm sure they would,' Meg murmured. She seized the salad bowl and hurried from the room before her mother could say anything more.

* * *

'You're one crazy guy, sir,' Ron joked as he collected Jago and his luggage from the hotel. 'I've never heard of anyone turning into a barbecue sauce magnate and buying a house and farm all in the same day. Are you going to propose to the pretty lady next door tomorrow?'

'Now who's the crazy one?' Jago retorted. 'I'm fancy-free and plan to stay that way.'

'Working well, is it?'

Jago didn't reply.

They joined in with the late-night traffic and headed out of the city.

Warren Green had worked wonders in a short time. They had a provisional contract in place, and the owner had no objection to Jago moving in immediately and paying rent until they closed the deal. Money definitely talked. He'd delayed his morning meeting with the new Mama Belle's board and persuaded Ron to work some overtime.

'You don't have to answer,' Ron said with a wink. 'We both know.'

'Have you signed up for any college classes yet?' Jago tossed back.

'Yeah, actually I have.' The triumph in Ron's eyes was unmistakeable. 'Starting in the fall.'

'Well done.'

'Are you going to step up too?'

'I'm thinking about it. Don't nag. You're worse than my mother.'

Ron chuckled. 'Probably because I know more than she does.'

True. He kept allowing his mother's phone calls to go to voicemail, but she deserved to hear about his new plans. 'I'll talk to her soon.'

'Before those pink pigs start flying?'

Jago succumbed to a smile. 'Let's go and see my new home.'

'Sounds good, sir.'

'It is.' Jago turned away to stare out of the window. He'd bared his soul enough for one day.

★ ★ ★

Meg held the phone out to her father. 'It's Guy Winters calling from Magnolia Glade.'

'Y'all excuse me a minute. Carry on playing and I'll be back.' He took the phone and walked out into the hall so he could hear above all the chatter going on. They were in the middle of a heated game of Scrabble and Meg went back to studying her letters.

'Really? Are you sure?'

Everybody stopped and listened. The Harper family didn't do discreet eavesdropping.

'I sure do.' Gray hesitated. 'I'll . . . come over in the morning, Guy.' He came back in and looked around at them all.

'Is something wrong?' Betty Lou asked.

'Not exactly.'

'What's up then? Spit it out.'

Gray fixed his attention on Cecily. 'That was the farm manager at Magnolia Glade — the property next to ours. Old Mr. Jordan died at the end of last year and a distant cousin in New York inherited. He put it up for sale, and apparently someone made an offer today. The man's already moved in on a temporary basis.'

'Why would Cecily care?' Meg asked.

'Maybe because Guy swears that Jago is the new owner.'

An awkward silence fell on the room.

'Jago?' Cecily whispered. 'You're joking.'

'Nope. They met a short while ago and Guy described him to me — it's definitely your boy.'

A curl of anger formed a knot in Meg's stomach.

'I suppose it makes sense for him to get somewhere proper to live if he's going to be working long-term with Mama Belle's.' Cecily put on a brave face but was clearly embarrassed.

'Sure it does.' Betty Lou reached over and patted the other woman's hand. 'It's great news. We'll get to see more of y'all when you come to visit him.'

'That's a bit of news, I must say. Are you ready for bed, love? I know I am.' Ernie put an arm around his wife's shoulder. Cecily nodded and no one said anything as they left.

'Well, fancy that!' Betty Lou exclaimed. 'I have to say that boy's gone down in my estimation.'

'Maybe he has a good reason not to say anything yet.' Gray played the peacemaker as his usual role.

Meg fumed. Her father had encouraged her to be honest to Jago about her feelings. She'd be honest all right, and he wouldn't care for it one bit.

24

The shrill doorbell disturbed Jago in the middle of searching for clean sheets for his bed. He guessed it was Guy Winters again. They'd hit it off instantly, and unless his enquiries tomorrow showed up anything untoward, he hoped the man would stay on to work for him. Guy had grown up on his parents' nearby farm before coming to work for the Jordan family five years ago, and although only thirty, he had a steadiness about him Jago appreciated.

'Meg! What on earth are you doing here?'

'I could ask you the same thing.' Her fierce glare and sharp tone of voice indicated she wasn't happy with him. Again. 'Tired of hotel life?'

'How about you come in and let me explain?'

'I will, but only because the bugs are

eating me alive out here.'

Jago stood to one side while she stepped into the dark, dingy hall. 'We could sit on the porch where it's a little cooler. I'm afraid the house is hot because the air conditioner needs replacing. I would offer you a cold drink, but there's nothing apart from lukewarm tap water.'

'You're certifiable. You do know that?'

'Maybe.' People had been telling him that ever since he was ten years old. That summer he'd raked in over a hundred pounds by selling cold bottles of water to tourists stuck in traffic near his house during a heat wave. He led the way out through the dingy lounge to the screened-in porch. The large room stuck on the back of the house was decorated in what Jago would call reject-style. Stray furniture had plainly been dumped there over the years and never moved again. Several massive ferns standing in heavy stone pots gave the area a peculiar musty wildness. Meg brushed off a dusty wicker chair and sat down.

'How did you find me?' He attempted to make a joke of it but she didn't smile.

'Out here in the country we know our neighbours. Our farm joins onto this one. My father knows Guy Winters well and they often talk. Question answered?'

A horrible realisation slammed into him. 'My mother.'

'Give the man an A.'

'It never occurred to me,' he groaned. 'I planned to ring her tomorrow and invite them over. I thought it'd be a happy surprise.'

Meg scoffed. 'It certainly was a surprise. You made her look like an idiot.'

'Oh Meghan, I never meant to do that. You know me better than that, surely?'

'I suppose.'

'Only suppose?'

'Fine. I know you didn't. All right?' Meg conceded.

'Do they know you're here now?'

She shook her head. 'I said I needed a few things at the shop in Leiper's Fork. I'm not sure my mom believed me, but she didn't ask any questions for once.' The faintest trace of a smile pulled at the corners of her mouth. 'Was this house an impulse buy?'

Jago considered how to answer. 'Yes and no. It's been in the back of my mind for a while to settle somewhere, and I spotted this property when I cycled to Franklin. When the Mama Belle's thing fell into place . . . it sort-of happened.'

Her eyebrows rose. 'You 'sort-of happened' to buy fifty-plus acres of land and a big family house right next door to my folks?'

Put that way, it sounded like a cross between mad and stalker-ish.

A sudden wave of tiredness swept over Meg.

'Long day?' Jago's low, velvety voice wrapped around her and mingled with the sultry evening air. He crouched down in front of her and cradled her face in his large hands. His fingers rubbed gentle rhythmic circles at her temples and worked miracles on her dull headache.

'You should franchise those hands.' A thick lock of his hair flopped forward, which Meg couldn't resist pushing out of the way.

'Not going to happen. They're reserved.'

'Who for?' She hardly dared to ask.

'The woman who's captured my heart and won't let go.'

'Do you want her to?'

'Want? Need? It seems I'm helpless against her.'

'She's helpless too, if that's any consolation,' Meg admitted with a sigh.

'Is she? Really?'

Meg managed to nod.

'Will you sit with me?' He stood up and gestured towards an ancient wooden swing hanging from the porch rafters. 'I think it'll hold us both.'

'Are you implying I'm heavy?'

'Give me a break. Please.'

'I'm only messing with you.' Meg hurried to reassure him and didn't protest when Jago took hold of her hand and led her across the porch. They sat together, and he kicked his foot to get the swing moving before wrapping his arm around her shoulders. For a few indulgent minutes she relished the simple pleasure of resting her head on Jago's chest while his heartbeat hummed through her blood.

'Your day?'

Meg dived in and told him about her meeting with Elliott in the park. 'I should be relieved . . . '

'But you're sad. You have a long history together.'

'I understand why he can't be friends with me anymore.'

'No, but that doesn't make it easy. Did anything else happen?'

'You aren't going to like this, but I told my parents about us meeting in Italy. It didn't feel right them not knowing,' Meg murmured. 'I'm sorry.'

'I'm not.'

'Really?'

'Yes, really.'

'But we didn't tell Cecily and Ernie,' Meg assured him. 'That's up to you.'

'Fair enough. I've a lot to talk to them about one way or another. I've been a fool.' He gave her a wry smile. 'This is when you're supposed to say I could never be such a thing.'

'I thought we were being honest with each now,' Meg replied, unable to stop grinning. 'Anyway, you're not the only foolish one.'

'Apparently not.'

'You're no gentleman,' she half-heartedly protested. Jago instantly silenced her with a long, delicious kiss.

'Do you want to risk saying that again?'

'I might if I get the same response.'

'Only might? I must be slipping.' Jago tightened his hold on Meg and kissed her again. 'You're a dangerous lady.' He pulled away. 'I'd better let you go home before I forget myself.'

Meg didn't say a word, but he gave

her a satisfied smile. Clearly he recognised the feelings she couldn't put into words yet.

'You'll come back tomorrow evening?'

'What about your folks?'

'I really need you here when I talk to them. I don't intend for you to be a grubby little secret any longer.' Jago swore under his breath. 'Sorry, that didn't come out the way I intended, as usual. It's only grubby because of my bad behaviour in standing you up in Italy. I wanted you too much and it scared me.'

Meg smiled. 'I know that now or I wouldn't be here. If I come straight here from work I might avoid any more questions from my parents.'

'I don't want you going behind their backs,' he said quietly. 'Tell them.'

'Thanks.'

They got up in silence and strolled back through the house. In the near-darkness, Jago kissed Meg again until she could barely breathe.

'All this time I thought Italy had

bewitched me, but now I know it was simply you.' Meg's rueful explanation made him smile.

'Good night.' She fumbled in her pocket for the car keys.

'Ring me when you get home.'

'I'm only going about a mile back down the road.'

'Doesn't matter. I look out for the people I care for.'

Does that include me?

'Yes.'

Jago's quiet answer to her unspoken question touched Meg. 'I'll call.' She blew him a kiss as she walked away with a new lightness in her step. Roll on tomorrow.

25

Jago checked out the grim faces of the men seated around the conference table. He'd promised them a turn-around in the company if they took his money, but so far they'd been at the discussions for two hours and made zero progress.

'You're the barbecue sauce experts and I know how to build a business,' he said. 'We can do this.'

'Really? I thought all you did was tear down companies and sell the scraps for a profit.'

Elliott's snide remark aggravated Jago's tense mood. He checked the time. 'How about we take a ten-minute coffee break for coffee?' he suggested, and gave his nemesis a tight smile. 'Would you mind joining me on the balcony? I need some air.'

Elliott opened his mouth to reply but

shut it again. Jago helped himself to coffee from the table at the back of the room and stepped out onto the narrow balcony overlooking Broadway.

Tourists were already flocking to the myriad shops and music venues lining the popular street. When the sun went down the ambiance changed, but now it was mainly families buying cowboy boots and T-shirts while they decided where to eat lunch.

'What's the problem?' Elliott said.

'You are.'

'Me?' Elliott's expression remained impassive. 'Why did you drag me out here? What do you want?'

Jago needed to play this carefully. 'Your grandfather was a founder of Mama Belle's, right?'

'Yeah. So what?'

'Do you intend to be the one to destroy his legacy?'

'Certainly not,' Elliott protested. 'Why do you think I agreed to you buying a share in the business?'

Jago fixed the other man with his best

intimidating stare. 'I don't know. Why don't you tell me? From where I'm standing you're doing all you can to sabotage my suggestions.'

'It's awkward.' He shifted in place and took a sip of his coffee. 'Can't you see how difficult this is for me?'

Finally they were getting somewhere. 'Yes, I can, and I'm sorry. But sorry won't stop you from going bankrupt. I can. You can either be part of the problem or part of the solution.' Jago ploughed on: 'I'd rather have you on board, but if you continue with this obstructive behaviour I'll table a motion to get you kicked off.'

'You wouldn't get away with it!' Elliott protested. 'These are *my* people. They'll back me against any outsider.'

He planted a kernel of doubt. 'Are you sure of that? They want to make a profit. Something to leave their children and grandchildren. I'm willing to bet a million dollars they'll throw you under the bus without a second thought.' Jago watched the wheels turn in Elliott's head.

'I don't want you to be right.'

'I know.'

'I've got a ton of ideas the sticks-in-the mud won't like,' Elliott warned.

'Good.' Jago made a swift decision. 'Let's go back in, and I'll propose that we end the meeting for today. Tomorrow morning I'm going to ask them all to come in and present three ideas for improving the business.'

'I expect Clayborne's suggestions will consist of offering to play a few more rounds of golf with his cronies,' Elliott joked.

'We'll let him. He'd be a danger anywhere else.' Jago smiled. 'I'm really after *your* ideas, but I think John Warner might do okay too, and Aaron Smith isn't a complete loss.'

'People usually mark me down as laid-back and happy to go along with the status quo. Why do you think differently?' Elliott's pale eyes narrowed.

'It's what I do, and one reason I've

been successful in business.' Jago told the story about his water bottle sales and Elliott cracked a smile. 'You've never been pushed before. It feels good, doesn't it?'

'I guess.'

Jago stuck out his hand. 'Are we on the same side?'

'I'm not over the whole thing with Meg yet, but leaving her aside — yeah, let's go for it.'

Jago didn't press the matter and they shook hands. 'Let's go out now for an early lunch and talk some more.'

'Okay,' Elliott agreed. 'We'll check out one of the barbecue places nearby to get the inspiration flowing.'

For the first time they laughed together. Meg would tear her hair out if they became friends, but stranger things had happened.

★   ★   ★

Meg longed to wipe the smug smile off her parents' faces that'd been there ever since she'd told them about her visit to Jago the previous night.

'I know it's early, but I'm going on over to Magnolia Glade before Cecily and Ernie get back from sightseeing. Jago wants me to be there when they arrive,' she said.

'Good idea,' her mother agreed. 'I'm glad the boy's come to his senses. Are you sure you don't want to take any food with you to help out? There's plenty here.'

'Thanks, but Jago assured me he'd arrange dinner. No doubt he'll order in pizza.' Meg laughed. 'I'd better go and change. I've been in this dress all day.'

'Did your meeting go well?' Gray asked.

'Yeah, it did. I've got my fingers crossed that Marvin Welles will choose me to work with him.' She was determined not to be caught out when she got her marching orders from Mama Belle's and had put out a few feelers around Nashville. At lunchtime she'd met up with the well-known country music singer whose career was in a slump. He'd liked the initial ideas she'd presented and promised to let her know his decision by the end of the week.

'The man will snatch you up if he's got any sense,' Gray said.

Meg gave him a quick kiss and hurried upstairs to her room.

After a refreshing shower she reapplied her make-up and stood in front of her closet in her clean underwear. Although Cecily and Ernie knew her well, she still wanted to make a good impression. Cecily claimed she wanted Jago to find a good woman, but that didn't mean she'd welcome just anyone to apply for the job.

Calm down. Don't put the proverbial cart before the horse.

Without knowing if Jago had got his air conditioning fixed, Meg chose the coolest outfit she owned. She'd made the sleeveless dress herself last month out of a fine sea-green cotton shot through with blue and silver, and tonight would be its debut. Paired with thin silver sandals, a simple jade necklace and silver drop earrings, it would hopefully strike the right balance between trying too hard and not hard enough.

She snatched her keys and phone from the table before running back downstairs, then yelled goodbye and hurried out of the front door. A few seconds later she clutched the steering wheel, counted to ten and turned the key one more time. Nothing. The new battery she'd bought last week was obviously a waste of money. She climbed back out and headed inside.

'Dad, can I borrow the truck? My car's not . . . ' Her voice petered out as she saw Cecily, Ernie and her parents all standing around the kitchen talking.

'Going somewhere nice?' Cecily asked.

There wasn't any point in lying. They'd see her again soon enough. 'Jago invited me to join y'all for dinner.'

'Really?' His mother couldn't hide

her surprise. 'Oh, how nice.'

'You can ride over with us,' Ernie said with a kind smile.

'Thank you.'

'We were just going to freshen up. He said to get there about six.'

'Perfect.' Meg must get a message to Jago or he might think she'd stood him up. Once his parents left, she stepped out onto the patio. 'Change of plan,' she said as soon as he answered. Meg rattled off a quick version of what had happened and Jago groaned. 'It can't be helped. Your mom is suspicious.'

'I wonder why. Oh well, I'll see you soon.' Meg spotted Ernie coming back downstairs. 'Got to go.' She rang off and plastered a smile on her face before walking back inside to face the music.

26

'So that's it, really.' Jago picked up Meg's hand and cradled it with his own, watching his mother's reaction closely.

'Told you so, didn't I?' Cecily flashed his step-father a triumphant smile.

'You sure did.' Ernie chuckled and shook his head at Jago. 'Fancy thinking you could hide anything from your mother. She swore the pair of you were up to something.'

Jago wasn't sure how to proceed, not wanting to imply either too much or too little.

'We're still working things out. We're not rushing into anything,' Meg said gently.

Jago tried to be grateful, but for a usually cautious man he had the wild urge to throw himself at Meg's feet and beg her to put in her lot with him.

Aren't you just the last of the great romantics. She wants to be wooed properly this time. You won't get a third chance.

'Very sensible,' his mother agreed. 'Now, tell me all about this house and why you bought it without a word to us, you naughty boy.'

Jago felt five years old again. He remembered wasting his pocket money on a model airplane kit his mother warned him was made of cheap flimsy wood. She said it would fall apart the first time he flew it, and she'd been right.

He picked his way cautiously around his future plans and sensed Meg listening closely to every word.

'Are you going to show us around?' his mother asked.

'Of course, but why don't we have dinner first?' he suggested.

'I don't smell anything cooking.'

He'd needed to get creative today. Guy Winters had come through for him and persuaded his sister and a couple of her friends to give the house a good clean. They'd set up electric fans in strategic spots to ease the stifling heat, stocked Jago up with some basic groceries, and added enough offerings from a local deli for him to pull off this impromptu dinner party.

'I've kept to all cold food because the air conditioner can't be replaced until the end of the week, so I thought we wouldn't want to get any hotter,' he explained. 'Why don't you and Ernie drink some more champagne while Meg helps me to set up everything in the dining room?' Jago turned to her. 'If you don't mind?'

'I'd be happy to.'

In the kitchen he closed the door with his foot and swept Meg into his arms for a long sweet kiss.

'Dinner?' Meg whispered.

'In a minute . . . or two. It won't take long.' He pressed a trail of soft kisses all the way down her neck. 'Will you'll stay after they leave and I'll take you home later?'

'That sounds perfect.'

'This is beautiful.' He ran his hand down over her dress, fingering the soft material. 'You look like an enticing mermaid.'

'You're poetic tonight,' Meg teased. 'I made it myself.'

'You did?'

'Yeah. Don't sound so surprised. I may not be a leather worker, but I do love to sew.'

'A woman of many talents,' Jago said with a broad smile. 'I suppose we'd better see to dinner or they'll be sending out a search party.' Reluctantly he let go of her and headed towards the fridge. 'Guy is pretty sure the owners didn't make any changes to the house after about 1970.'

'He's probably right. I haven't been inside here for years. Mr. and Mrs. Jordan weren't very social, and when she passed away he struggled on alone. Mom would come over occasionally and bring him food, but he always refused any other help.'

Jago pulled out several plastic-covered dishes and set them on the old kitchen table that was still covered in the original sky-blue Formica. 'You'll find paper plates, disposable cutlery and plastic glasses in there already.' He touched her arm. 'There are a couple of things I want to talk to you about later.' He needed to be honest about Elliott, plus there was the question of his father. He'd picked up Marco's business card multiple times and stared at it without coming to any decision. Jago knew in his heart what Meg's opinion would be.

'That sounds serious.'

'It is, but it's not bad . . . more complicated.'

'Tell me everything when we're on our own.'

'I will do,' he promised. 'Let's get this show on the road.'

*   *   *

Meg fell under the weave of Jago's spell again as the witty, charming man she'd fallen for in Florence stepped back out of the shadows. After a delicious meal, they took a long tour around the house and swapped ideas for what improvements to make. Finally Cecily stifled a yawn.

'Goodness, I'm sorry,' she apologised, and glanced at her husband. 'I think we'd better make a move.'

'Fair enough. Are you ready, Meg?'

Jago hitched his arm around her shoulder. 'I can't let you take her away this early. I'll see her home safely later.'

The four of them made their way back through the house and gathered at the front door. Cecily gave Meg a hug. 'I hope my idiotic son has the sense to get it right this time.'

'Ceci, what did we agree?' Ernie complained.

'I know you think it's none of my business, but he's my boy, and I want to see him happy. All the money he's made hasn't done the trick, and he's lonely,' she insisted, tilting her chin in the air.

'I'm sorry about this,' Ernie groaned. 'She's tired and — '

'Don't apologise for me. I meant every word.'

'Yes, she did, and it's all good,' Jago suddenly spoke up. 'She's absolutely right.'

Meg couldn't believe what she was hearing. She'd expected him to be mortified, but he recognised the comment for what it was — the truth spoken out of love.

'I'll do my best, Mum, okay?' He hugged his mother.

'I know you will. You always do.' Cecily straightened up and glanced at Ernie. 'Take me to bed.'

'Happily.' Ernie's heartfelt reply made everyone laugh.

A few minutes later, Jago and Meg were finally alone. 'Don't say anything for a minute, sweetheart.' Jago tightened his arms around her and plastered her up against his warm, broad chest. 'We deserve this.' He chuckled. 'Mothers, eh?'

'Mine's just as bad. She and my dad are walking around with abominably satisfying grins on their faces.'

'I suppose we'll understand better one day when . . . ' He stopped and a flame of heat zoomed up his neck. 'I meant, um . . . nothing.'

'Yes, of course you meant absolutely nothing,' Meg teased. They both knew he'd been about to say something it was far too soon for.

'Let's go inside and talk.' He grimaced. 'I know that will be torture for you, but I'm like that.'

'I'd noticed, you spoilsport.'

They sat on their new favourite porch swing and Meg snuggled into Jago. 'You're not getting rid of this old thing. You can mend and repaint it, but that's all.'

'Bossy woman.'

'Have you got a problem with that?'

'Not in the least. You've seen my mother in full flow. I love strong women.'

'Good.' She didn't try to hide her

satisfaction. 'Now, talk.'

Jago stroked her hair. 'I need you to listen carefully before you give me your opinion, and please don't get defensive. This isn't about you.'

Meg's heart thumped in her chest. What on earth was he going to tell her?

27

'Elliott and I have come to an understanding.'

'Wonderful! Has he given us his blessing?' Sarcasm gushed out of her and Jago prepared for an uphill battle.

'What did I say a minute ago?'

'This isn't about me,' she muttered.

'Right.' Jago quickly poured out the whole story of the frustration he'd felt at the board meeting, the challenge he'd made to Elliott, and the other man's surprising reaction. 'I need him on my side, Meg. He's the future of the business. When he came down off his high horse, he had some great ideas.' He expanded on everything they'd talked about over lunch, and Meg's eyes widened.

'Elliott thought of all that?'

'Is that so impossible to believe?'

'It is to someone who couldn't get

him to choose between blue or gray paint for the bedroom walls when I helped him to redecorate his apartment.' She gave Jago a shrewd stare. 'You're good for him. He always let me make all of the decisions, but I came to resent him for it.'

'Why do you think he responded to me?'

'For a start he's not in love with you.' Meg chuckled. 'In fact probably the opposite. All his life he's been stuck with the label of being good-looking and affable. He's relied on those things to get him through life, but you came in with no preconceived views and found his hidden strengths.'

'Do you mind?'

'Mind?' She frowned. ''Mind' isn't the right word. I'm maybe a little sad because I never saw that in him. I'm happy for Elliott because he deserves more from life, plus I want the business to succeed. Mama Belle's sauce is a great product and deserves to stick around.'

'One thing he said shook me from the ground up, though, and I still can't believe he had the guts to suggest it.'

'What are you talking about?'

'He said we can streamline production and be more efficient, but if no one buys the sauce we're sunk. He insisted there's no one better than you at public relations, so we need to keep you in the business to do all the marketing and advertising for Mama Belle's. He even suggested giving you a seat on the board if things go well.'

'Me?' Meg gasped. 'Elliott said he couldn't possibly remain friends with me, but now he wants to continue to work together? Has he gone totally crazy?'

Jago understood where she was coming from and wasn't sure how to reply.

'Do you seriously think it could work?' she asked. 'What if I slip back into bossing him around again?'

'I won't let you,' Jago said with a

broad grin. 'How about you come and talk to the board tomorrow about your ideas and see how they react?'

'I'm not sure,' Meg murmured. 'I've tried hard for the last year and got nowhere.'

'I can't promise things will be different, but I think you might be pleasantly surprised.'

She straightened back her shoulders. 'Okay. You're on. We'll give it another try.'

I love you, you amazing woman. Instead of saying it out loud he kissed her, pouring into his kiss everything he couldn't put into words.

'Mm.' Meg sighed. 'I could do this all night.'

'But?'

'Is that all you wanted to hash out?'

Being understood so well was a double-edged sword. Right now it left him with nowhere to hide.

'You don't have to tell me if you're not ready.'

'I need to,' Jago assured her. 'I've

kept it to myself for the best part of a week and it's eating me up.' The colour drained from Meg's skin. 'Honey, it's nothing to do with us, honestly.'

'Are you sure? The last time you left me without a word, I . . . ' Meg's voice faltered.

'I would never do that again. I was a stupid fool. I love you.' The confession poured out of him, and he couldn't regret a word when a radiant smile lit up her face. 'Sorry. I meant to be more romantic when I finally got up the nerve to tell you.'

'Don't fret. 'Genuine and honest' trumps any sort of hearts-and-flowers romance any day.' Meg gave an impish smile. 'Of course I won't turn down a little romance as well.'

He wrapped her in a tight hug. 'You'd better turn it down if it's not coming from me.'

'You'll have to keep me happy then, won't you?' she jibed.

Jago's throat tightened around the promise he desperately wanted to make. 'I think we've both had enough for one night, don't you?'

Once again she was right. Between sorting things out with his mother and laying his emotions on the line with Meg, he was drained. They could discuss their future another day, and he'd tell her then about his father.

'Why don't you come over to Red Roof for dinner tomorrow night and we'll make sure to get some time on our own afterwards?'

'That sounds perfect. You're a good woman. The best.' In his head he added, *And you're mine*. One day soon he'd make it official.

★   ★   ★

Meg woke up with her alarm clock buzzing and someone banging on the door. She hated to leave the delicious dream she'd been having involving Jago, red roses and a glittering diamond ring.

'What?' she yelled.

'Your boyfriend and his fancy chauffeur-driven car are waiting for you.'

'Why?' Meg stumbled from the bed and opened the door to her grinning father.

'Jago says he promised you a lift to work because your car is out of commission. I didn't mention that we have several spare cars around the place.' He glanced down at her pyjamas. 'I could get your mother to feed them while you shower and dress if it'd help?'

'You'd better ask if that's okay first. Jago might be in a hurry.'

Gray chuckled. 'He'll wait. The man's got it bad. It's written all over him.'

Meg struggled to hide her pleasure. 'Thanks, Dad.' She kissed him and closed the door. Out of the blue she thought about Elliott, and a dark cloud spread over the day. Maybe she'd been reckless to consider working with him again. *Don't get ahead of yourself. See what happens.*

After her shower, Meg considered what to wear. Her hand hovered over a pretty pink-and-white summer dress Jago would love, but instead she selected her black suit. It would help the board members to take her more seriously. She wasn't a public relations guru for nothing. She checked her appearance in the mirror, smoothed down her hair one last time, and added a slick of deep red lipstick. Discreet was one thing; boring quite another.

'Sorry to keep you waiting,' Meg said as she breezed into the kitchen, and stopped in her tracks at the sight of Jago. He'd slicked back his black hair, enhancing the severity of his charcoal-gray suit, white shirt, and dark green silk tie. Her stomach fluttered because he looked a million miles from her laid-back Italian Romeo this morning; but as Jago held her gaze the flitters of panic disappeared. 'I'll fix my coffee and bring it with me.'

'We can hold off on leaving while you get something to eat.'

Meg didn't want to admit in front of everyone that she couldn't swallow a thing until she got this meeting over with. 'That's not necessary. I'm not much of a breakfast eater.' She suddenly became aware that their parents were there. 'Heck, you're all up early today.' *All the better to check us out.*

'I've been pestering Jago to tell me what he'd like me to cook for dinner tonight,' Betty Lou said. 'He heard me braggin' about my spaghetti and meatballs the other day, so I'm making them later.'

Meg concentrated on making sure the top was on her thermal coffee mug. She didn't dare look at her father. As far as most things were concerned, her mother was an amazing cook. Her light, fluffy biscuits were the things dreams were made of, and nobody made better fried chicken. But her meatballs were another story. In bygone days they would've been used as medieval cannon fodder, but her family had never been able to hurt her feelings by telling the truth. She plastered on a smile. 'That's wonderful,' she said, ostentatiously checking her watch. 'We'd better be going. See y'all tonight.' She snatched her laptop bag from the counter and headed for the door.

Jago hurried to catch up. 'Did I do something wrong?'

'Wrong?' Meg grinned. 'Not exactly, although your stomach might disagree tomorrow.'

'You're talking in riddles.'

As they walked out to the car, she quickly explained about the stone-in-your-gut meatballs. 'Trust me, there's a good reason why none of us ever ask for them. We force them down once a year as a penance for all the other great stuff she cooks.'

'I thought I noticed your dad wince when I made the request. Sorry.' Jago's good-humoured apology made her laugh. Finally he gave Meg the hug she'd been craving.

Ron hopped out of the car and

opened the back door. 'Behave yourself, sir, and take your hands off the poor woman. You'll get her all wrinkled, and they don't like that.'

'Remind me again why you're still my driver and I haven't bought my own car yet?' Jago retorted.

'Two good reasons. You appreciate my wit and candour, plus you're wary of driving on the wrong side of the road. Just having that rental car the other day freaked you out.'

A tinge of colour reddened Jago's skin. Meg couldn't imagine this smart, competent man being fazed by anything, but everyone had their weak spots.

'Let's go.' Jago gestured towards the car. 'I'll sit up front to make sure Ron doesn't take a wrong turn and head to Canada instead.' He ushered Meg into the back seat and closed her door before getting in himself. 'Nashville next stop — and no more smart remarks, Mr. Weber.'

'Yes sir, Mr. Merryn sir.' The driver

flipped an exaggerated salute and his loud, rich laughter filled the car as they drove away.

Meg rested back against the seat and gazed out of the window. She tried not think about facing Elliott again, but her apprehension flooded back with a vengeance.

28

'Are you doing okay?' Jago squeezed Meg's hand as they walked into the building. 'I'm sure you'll wow them.'

Last night he'd given a lot of thought to the best way to manage things this morning and decided he must treat the meeting exactly the same as he would any other. Meg could start things off by presenting her ideas in front of the whole group, and he'd chair the ensuing discussion. The question haunting him was whether his business ambitions were blinding him to the uneasy triangle between himself, Meg, and Elliott. He guessed he wouldn't know until they were in the same room together.

'I'm not good at this.' He hesitated on the top step.

'What?'

'Mixing my business and personal

lives. I want to do right by you, but I must do the best for the company too.'

'You will,' Meg assured him, 'and I want exactly the same. Elliott and I are grown-ups. If he's prepared to give this a go, I am too.'

The determined tilt to her chin emboldened Jago, and he couldn't resist brushing a light kiss over her cheek. 'You're a star. Come on.' He followed her upstairs. 'Why don't you wait out here for a minute while I have a word with the board first? Our main task this morning is to win over anyone who's sitting on the fence where change is concerned.'

'I can be very persuasive.'

'Oh, I know that,' he joked.

'Behave yourself. Let's get this done.'

Jago nodded and headed into the boardroom.

★ ★ ★

Meg put on her brightest smile and looked around the room in a friendly challenge. The subtle difference in the balance of power emboldened her, and she got the impression of having been listened to carefully for the first time.

'You've heard my ideas, gentlemen, and now I'd like to hear yours.' No one spoke, and Meg decided to pick on the one person apart from Jago who was supposed to be supporting her. 'Elliott, I understand you have some interesting concepts in mind.' The tips of his ears turned pink, a sure sign he was embarrassed. *Get over it, Elliott, and prove Jago right. I'd better not have come here to be made a fool of.*

'Yes, I do.' The new level of sureness in his voice surprised her. 'We can't compete with the big boys in the industry and we don't need to try. The buzz concepts at the moment are anything handmade, artisanal, and traditional but done with a modern twist. We need to play up our long history and appeal to discerning customers who are searching for something unique. I suggest for a start that we create limited quantities of sauce to make it sought-after.'

'You've nailed it.' Meg didn't try to hide her enthusiasm. 'I wondered about getting an old-school, well-respected country singer on our side, because that'll carry a lot around the south.' She already had someone in mind. Marvin Welles, with his craggy face, long white beard, and deep rugged voice, would be ideal for the job.

'How about using some of the older workers who've been with us forever in a commercial? Play up the whole continuity side of the business,' John Warner suggested.

'That's a great idea,' Meg agreed.

'All the young up-and-coming chefs in Nashville are touting the farm-to-table concept,' Aaron Smith spoke up from the back of the room. 'They're into organic, sustainable farming, and Mama Belle's has been all-natural from day one. If we can convince one of those chefs to use our sauce exclusively in their restaurant, it'll bring in a whole new group of customers.'

Meg beamed. 'That's — '

'A load of bull,' Clayborne Williams blustered. 'What's wrong with letting a good product speak for itself?'

Before Meg could answer, Elliott jumped in. 'Because that doesn't cut it these days, if it ever did. That kind of attitude is why we're in this position in the first place. Mr. Merryn hasn't handed over a stack of money so we can continue to run a good business into the ground. If you can't contribute anything useful, at least allow those of us who really care to steer Mama Belle's back on track.'

'You young whipper-snapper, who do you think you're talking to? Your grandfather would roll over in his grave,' Williams retorted.

'He'll jump up out of it if you let Mama Belle's go under because you're too stubborn to make the changes we need to survive.'

Jago raised his hand. 'All right everyone, that's enough. We've obviously got a lot to talk about, but the first order of business is whether everyone is happy to keep Ms. Harper as the new head of advertising and marketing. I'll ask her to wait outside while we take a vote.' His firm tone made it clear he wouldn't allow the meeting to degenerate into a slanging match. 'If you wouldn't mind, Meg.'

'Of course.' She left and paced up and down the narrow corridor. She practically jumped out of her skin when Jago opened the door and stepped out to join her.

'Would you care to come back in?' His bland expression revealed nothing.

'Thank you.'

He lowered his voice. 'Don't get cross, but I came clean about our personal relationship.'

'Why?'

'Because I don't want any comebacks later. I hold myself and anyone I do business with to strict ethical standards. I'm tough, but I always strive to be honest and fair.'

Meg might not like it, but he was right. His father's broken promises had left behind a bitter legacy, but in many ways they'd shaped Jago into the man he was today. 'How did they react?'

'There were a few raised eyebrows.' He frowned. 'I should've warned Elliott, but he handled it well.'

'Good.'

'Am I forgiven?'

'Of course.' She kissed his cheek. 'Come on, let's go and hear the bad news.'

'Why do you assume it's bad?'

Meg shrugged. 'I'm guessing they won't want the complications I bring with me, and you're far more important to the business than I am.'

His eyes glittered. 'Maybe they're like me and enjoy complicated.'

'Maybe. Let's go and find out.'

'I already know.'

'Spoilsport.' Meg stuck out her tongue.

'That's no way to talk to your new boss.'

'New boss!' She stifled a squeal. 'Seriously? I won't let you down. Mama Belle's will be the most talked-about barbecue sauce in the south when I'm through.'

'I know.' His quiet certainty touched her. 'In you go, Ms. Harper.' He stepped to one side.

'Thank you, Mr. Merryn.'

They exchanged smiles and went in together.

*   *   *

'Any idea who the car belongs to?' Jago had spotted an old pick-up truck parked outside Meg's front door. He'd almost asked Ron to stop first at Magnolia Glade to allow him time to change out of his suit but didn't want to be responsible for Meg exploding from excitement. Ever since he had announced the board's decision, she'd been on cloud nine.

'No clue. Probably one of Dad's farming friends.' She turned to thank

261

Ron. 'Go on home to your family. We'll see he gets back safely tonight.'

'I'm not a five-year-old being dropped off at a birthday party,' Jago protested, but they both ignored him.

'You can pick him up in the morning whatever time his lordship desires. You know what these Brits are like,' Meg joked.

Ron rolled his eyes. 'Only too well, ma'am.'

'Let's say eight o'clock tomorrow,' Jago said. 'If that suits you, of course.' He ignored his driver's fake bow and made a grab for Meg's arm. 'Come on. Let's go and face your mother's meatballs.'

She groaned. 'I'd forgotten. And I've had such a good day, too.'

'I'll make up for it later.' Jago kissed her neck until she giggled and ordered him to behave himself.

She wriggled from his grasp and took off running, leaving him to trail behind carrying both of their computer bags. Jago reached the open front door and instantly froze at the sound of a gruff male voice drifting out from the kitchen. He should've known his father wouldn't keep his promise.

29

'What's wrong?' Meg pleaded, shaken by Jago's stony expression.

'There you are,' said her mother, bustling out into the hall. 'I hoped you wouldn't be late.'

'We said we'd be here by five. What's up?' She glanced between them both and sensed something she wasn't being told.

'We've got a . . . visitor.'

'So I hear,' Jago grunted.

'You know who it is?' Betty Lou asked.

'Oh yes.'

'Will someone please tell me what's going on?' Meg demanded, but Jago didn't answer straight away. He shrugged off his suit jacket and threw it on top of their bags on the floor. With silent deliberation, he undid his tie and added it to the pile before undoing the top button of his shirt and rolling up his sleeves.

'My father's here.'

'Your father! But I thought — '

'I did try to tell you.' *I've kept it to myself for the best part of a week and it's eating me up.*

'Oh God, I'm sorry.' Meg stepped closer and rested her head against his shoulder.

'Your mom's not taking it real well,' Betty Lou explained.

'I don't suppose she is,' Jago said. 'I should've told her. This is my fault.'

'No it's not,' Meg stated firmly. 'If anyone's to blame, it's your father.' She pulled away and then linked her arm through his. 'Let's go on through so I can meet him.' She lowered her voice. 'Remember I love you. I'm on your side.'

'That means a lot.'

Meg's heart raced as they walked together through the house. The tableau facing them in the kitchen could have been the setting for a stage play.

Cecily, her face white and strained, sat at the kitchen table with her husband standing protectively behind her. Betty Lou was now stirring a pot on the stove, and her father lingered by the back door, plainly ready to make a quick escape if necessary.

The man sitting across the table from Cecily struggled to his feet. He hadn't passed on his short stocky build to his son, but his dark wavy hair, olive Mediterranean skin and deep brown eyes were all quintessentially Jago. Meg made some rough calculations in her head and realised he was barely sixty, but his worn appearance hinted at a hard life.

'Jago.' Cecily's crisp voice cut through the awkward silence. 'Why don't you introduce Meg to your father. I understand *you've* seen each other recently.'

'Don't blame the boy.' Marco Raffaele held out his hands in a gesture of supplication. 'If it's any consolation, he tossed me out.'

'I thought you said if I changed my mind and wanted to contact you, I could. What happened?' Jago waved his arm around the crowded room. 'Do you call this giving me a choice? How did you find us here?'

His father swayed on his feet, and Gray pulled out a chair before helping him to sit down. 'Take it easy, son, he's not well.'

'And I'm supposed to care?'

Gray fixed his stern gaze on him. 'Yes, you are. He's still your father and deserves your respect. We all make mistakes.'

'You're wrong, Mr. Harper. I don't deserve anything but my son's contempt.' Against his will his father's despondent words touched Jago's heart. 'It wasn't difficult to find you. It only took a few phone calls. Hear me out for five minutes, and then I promise I'll leave. Please.' A wracking cough took hold of him and he struggled to catch his breath.

'Fine.' Jago pulled out a chair for

Meg and one for himself. 'Five minutes.'

'I don't intend to rehash the mess I made of your life and your dear mother's.' Marco's accent thickened, and Jago's mind filled with childhood memories of his father teaching him snippets of Italian when his mother wasn't around. 'I can't change what happened. I truly am sorry, but I'm well aware that means little or nothing now.'

'It actually means a lot to me,' Cecily interrupted, and Jago stared at her in shock. 'I believe you're telling the truth.'

'I am. It's been a long road.'

Jago kept quiet, and for the first time ever heard his parents speak to each without shouting. His father's story wasn't pretty. After he'd returned to Naples, he'd spiralled into depression and often been unemployed and homeless. Eventually he'd managed to claw his way back to a decent life. A reluctant admiration for his father's strength took hold of Jago and tears pricked at his eyes.

'I met a good woman and she saved me. You'd like Bella.'

'I'm sure I would.'

'I work with the homeless in Napoli, but I've been in America for a month now travelling around several different cities. I'm studying the problems you face here and the solutions you've come up with.'

'I always wanted to believe I wasn't wrong about you all those years ago,' Cecily half-whispered. 'I'm glad you've proved me right.' She leaned across the table and covered Marco's hand with her own. 'Is your cough serious?'

'Yes and no. I mix with a lot of sick people and I'm not as strong as I would like to be.' He shrugged. 'The doctors tell me to take it easy, but I have work to do. I do not intend to waste any more of my life. I'm flying back to Napoli tomorrow,' Marco said quietly. 'That's why I had to try one last time tonight.'

'I'm glad you did,' Jago blurted out.

'Seriously?'

'Yes. I almost got back in touch after I saw you last week, but it would've hurt my mother too much.'

'Oh, Jago.' Cecily's eyes filled with tears. 'I shouldn't have been so harsh when you were growing up, but I was so afraid you'd go in the same direction.'

'Don't you ever apologise,' he tried to reassure her. 'You did your very best.' Jago turned back to face his father again. 'I expect they've told you I bought the farm next door. I hope you'll come back for a visit when I'm settled in.'

'Really?'

'Yes.' Jago put his arm around Meg. 'We'd love you to.'

'We? Do you have plans for this beautiful young lady, Lucca?' A wide smile creased his father's face.

Jago wasn't sure how to answer.

'We certainly do,' Meg spoke up, and Jago stared at her in bemused disbelief. 'They're not set in stone yet, but we're going to work together on reinvigorating a local barbecue sauce company.' A teasing smile tugged at her mouth. 'I hope we'll be working together on a lot more in the future, but we'll leave it there for now.'

Jago's stunned silence must've registered because she suddenly gave him a gentle kiss on the cheek. 'Does that work for you?'

He nodded, beyond caring what he'd actually agreed to.

'OK then, dinner's ready.' Betty Lou beamed and clapped her hands. 'Gray, open the champagne we've been saving for a special occasion.' She touched Marco's shoulder. 'I insist that you stay and eat with us. I must've known you were coming, because I made my family's favourite Italian meatballs today.'

'Ah, meatballs! You are *bellissima*, Signora Harper.'

'He'll be calling her something far less charming when he's suffering from acute indigestion in the middle of the night,' Meg whispered in Jago's ear.

'Let that poor man alone for two seconds, Meghan Harper, and come and help me dish up.'

'Yes, Mom.'

The conversation returned to normal topics but Jago didn't join in. He sat quietly and watched the woman he loved more than life itself, together with the father he hadn't expected to ever see again. Even the prospect of tackling inedible meatballs couldn't put a dent in his good mood.

30

One year later

'It's still beyond me why you wouldn't agree to serving barbecue at our wedding reception,' Jago teased, pulling Meg closer to him on the porch swing. He'd sanded it down and painted the seat her favourite shade of duck-egg blue before rehanging the swing with new brass chains.

'Maybe because we've eaten, breathed and lived Mama Belle's for the last twelve months, and tomorrow is all about us. I'm not complaining, though, because it's been an amazing ride.'

'It certainly has,' he agreed. 'I saw Marvin Welles yesterday and he had a good laugh telling me about his fan club. Apparently he's got all these young girls swooning over him, along with their mothers who remember him from twenty years ago. He's having a ball.'

'I did pretty good there, didn't I?' Meg preened a little and then laughed at herself.

'You certainly did. The buzz around Nashville is that Marvin's new album is on track to hit number one in the country charts next week.'

'I get a kick every time I see his picture up on one of the billboards around Nashville as the face of Mama Belle's,' Meg mused. 'I forgot to tell you Elliott spotted one in New York last week when he was up there for the trade show. He did a great job pulling in more orders.' She patted Jago's hand. 'You were completely right about him, and I couldn't be happier.'

'You're not the only one who's pleased. I wasn't sure we'd pull it off.' He smiled. 'I've heard a rumour that he's been seen out on the town with Marvin's daughter, Briony.'

'Wow! That'll put the cat among the

pigeons,' Meg said, bursting into a raucous laugh. 'Elliott's mother is a real stickler for tradition and will only be happy with someone from a suitable old Nashville family for her beloved son. I hope it works out. Briony would be good for him. Oh, by the way, we should see another boost in our sales after Brad Donelson is featured on the *Today Show* on Wednesday. We'll have to get someone to record it for us.'

'Out of all the young Nashville chefs to talk into using our sauce in their restaurant, you picked the best — again.' A wave of emotion swept over Jago and he struggled to get his words out. 'You know that none of this business success means anything without you. I can't believe by this time tomorrow you'll be Mrs. Merryn.'

'Me neither, but doesn't it sound wonderful?'

'Certainly does.'

Meg rested her head on his shoulder. 'I suppose I ought to go home, or before we know it my mom will order my poor father to drive over here and haul me back. She's driven us all close to madness this week with trying to get everything perfect for the wedding.'

'My father's almost as bad.' Jago touched the sleeve of her soft green-and-white floral dress. 'I'm glad to see you're good at following orders.' Marco had insisted that the bride-to-be must wear something green on the evening before the wedding. 'I'd no idea there were so many Italian wedding traditions. They're certainly a superstitious people.' He cracked a wry smile. 'He should be happy. We've gone along with his insistence on a Sunday wedding for the best possible luck. Your wedding bouquet will arrive in the morning — ordered and paid for by me. Plus he's given me a small chunk of iron for in my pocket to ward off evil spirits. I think we've got all the bases covered, as you say here.'

'And Mom and I finished putting together the sugar-coated almond favours last night, and I think I can even pronounce them correctly now. *Bomboniere.*'

'Very good. By the time we get to Italy you'll be fluent,' Jago joked.

'We followed your father's instructions and put five almonds in each bag because we all know it's bad luck to have an even number. I'm beyond pleased he's going to be your best man.'

'Me too. I wouldn't have believed it a year ago, but there are a lot of other things I wouldn't have believed, so it's all good.' He gave her another lingering kiss. 'Are you happy with the way the house is shaping up?' When he hadn't been busy bringing the sauce factory into the twenty-first century, Jago had spent all of his time putting into effect Meg's renovation ideas for Magnolia Glade. They'd knocked down several internal walls to give a sense of light, and modernised throughout while retaining as many of the authentic features from the original design as possible.

'It's perfect and I can't wait to move in.'

'I'm counting the minutes too.' Jago played with her dark silky hair, which was longer now than usual because she apparently intended to do something fancy with it tomorrow. He hadn't been stupid enough to ask for any details.

'Oh, I embarrassed poor Guy this afternoon.' Meg giggled. 'I went outside for a walk around the vegetable garden and caught him showing a pretty woman around.'

'Kristin Gentry?'

'How do you know *everything*?' She playfully poked his arm.

'I came home from work one day last week and found her helping him with the mowing. If he plays his cards right, I'm pretty sure you'll have female company around here before too long. I would've mentioned seeing her, but we've hardly had a moment to breathe, let alone talk.'

Meg fell silent.

'Is it my turn to say I'm not

complaining?' Jago asked.

'Oh no, it's not that.' She gazed into his dark, serious eyes. 'I'm not mad. I simply started to think again about Monday and how I can hardly wait to get on that plane to Rome for our honeymoon.' She smiled. 'Or *luna de miele*, if we're getting into the spirit of Italy. A whole month travelling around Europe and doing exactly what we want. It's going to be blissful.'

'Oh, it will be.' Jago cradled her face with his hands. 'Do you know, it's about twenty-three hours and counting before I get you to myself for good? I'm thankful we won't have to travel far after the reception. It was a brilliant idea of mine to suggest holding the wedding at Red Roof Farm before coming here for our wedding night.'

Meg sighed happily as he stroked his finger down over her warm skin. 'We all know you're full of good ideas.' He eased away, his eyes dark with regret. 'You're going to send me home, aren't you?' she complained.

'I have to, honey. In another . . . ' He checked his watch. ' . . . thirty-two minutes, I'd be guilty of seeing you on our wedding day before the ceremony. According to our parents, the sky will fall if that happens.'

'We don't want to tempt fate, especially after we did that once in Italy and nearly lost each other. I'm not risking it again.' Meg's emphatic statement made him smile. She slid off the swing and held out her hand. 'Come on.'

They walked down the steps together and made their way around the front of the house to her car.

'Look.' Meg pointed up to the sparkling night sky. 'It's the last time we'll see the stars as single people. Pick the brightest one and make a wish.'

'What if I've got all I want already?'

'It can't hurt.' She grasped his hands and closed her eyes. 'Don't cheat. Close yours too.'

In the silence, Jago's heart beat against hers, and an overwhelming sensation of this moment marking the beginning of the rest of their lives together swept through her.

'You need to go and get some sleep or you'll look terrible in the pictures tomorrow,' she told him.

'It's not going to matter, sweetheart. Everyone will be looking at you. The groom's an afterthought.'

She scoffed. 'Not tomorrow he isn't. It's not my day or yours — it's ours.'

'I'll do as I'm told, I promise. But only after this.' Jago pulled Meg back into his arms and proceeded to kiss her until her head spun. Finally he let go and gave a satisfied nod. 'That should hold us over until about half-past twelve tomorrow.'

'What do you mean?'

'I timed it at the rehearsal today, and that should be about the time when the minister gets to the 'you may now kiss the bride' part of the ceremony. I don't intend to give you one of those polite 'everyone's watching' kisses, either. That's not good enough for *my* bride.'

A delightful shiver ran through Meg. *My bride*. This man would love her, protect her, and be her partner in every way. Out of all the people in the world, they'd been lucky enough to find each other a second time. They were living proof that wishes could come true.

'Those stars know what they're doing,' Meg whispered.